Anonymous

Byeways of Two Cities

Anonymous

Byeways of Two Cities

ISBN/EAN: 9783337405915

Printed in Europe, USA, Canada, Australia, Japan

Cover: Foto ©Andreas Hilbeck / pixelio.de

More available books at **www.hansebooks.com**

Byeways of Two Cities.

BY THE AUTHOR OF

"THE ROMANCE OF THE STREETS,"

ETC., ETC.

With a Prefatory Notice by the

RIGHT HON. THE EARL OF SHAFTESBURY, K.G.

London:

HODDER AND STOUGHTON,

PATERNOSTER ROW.

1873.

Several of the chapters of this work having previously appeared in a well-known periodical, some editorial notes by Mr. Spurgeon have been retained.

UNWIN BROTHERS, PRINTERS BY WATER POWER, CHILWORTH, SURREY.

CONTENTS.

PREFACE .. ..   PAGE 1

Part 1.—London.

I.

GOLDEN LANE 11

II.

THE. TAVERNS OF PADDINGTON .. .. ., 67

III.

JEWS AND SABBATH MARKETERS 139

viii

CONTENTS.

IV.

INFIDELITY IN LONDON 179

V.

LONDON ROUGHS 215

Part 2.—Edinburgh.

I.

A DAY WITH THE MEDICAL MISSION 241

II.

SUNDAY NIGHT IN THE COWGATE 275

PREFACE.

THE Author of the following pages is one of those valuable men—abundant now, compared with the past—who, by devoting their talents and their energies to the investigation of human life—particularly in its lowest forms—contribute largely to enlighten the public mind on the perils that threaten society, and on the remedies that may yet be applied to them.

I first had the pleasure of making his

acquaintance at a Costermongers' Meeting in Golden Lane—of which fraternity I am, myself, a member,—and I received from him, then, a book called 'The Romance of the Streets.' The present volume is a continuance of those narratives, lively, forcible, picturesque, and true; in which last expression lies a mighty claim on all, for its purchase and perusal.

A claim, I maintain, is conveyed in the word 'true'—for though I admit the great and lasting benefit conferred by Charles Dickens in his accurate and unrivalled representations of the poorer classes, and his unbounded sympathy for suffering humanity; yet they rested on a general experience, and appeared in the form of fiction. Here, on the contrary, the statements are facts ; and if we go into the districts specified, one will see the very people, hear the very words, and stand on the very spots, set out in detail in the work before us.

Most persons have read ' Poor Jack,' by the celebrated De Foe—a wonderful work, collectively true as to its several instances, though perhaps not the history of a single individual. If De Foe had found, in his day, a response to his appeal on behalf of neglected children, such as we hope may yet be found in ours, England would have been spared much sorrow and much degradation.

Now, one conclusion that we must, all of us, arrive at, either after reading these papers, or by visiting the people themselves—I answer at least for myself

—is that, looking to all the hopes of time and of eternity, we discover as good materials for labour and for harvest, among these forgotten classes, as we see in any other condition of life.

The pursuit of knowledge under difficulties has always been bepraised—and justly so—but why should not the pursuit of an honest livelihood amid great temptations be alike admired? Both are great moral efforts,—but I am inclined to think that the poor painstaking Costermonger, proof against enticements to fraud and falsehood, is, on the whole, the better citizen of the two. Literature may adorn a nation, but the uprightness of its citizens is its bulwark.

These records, and those by other writers in the same field, such as Mr.

Weylland, of the London City Mission,* exhibit the presence and influence of industry, perseverance, intelligence, and probity, to a far larger extent, among the rougher tribes of London, than most people are aware of. All these qualities may be called forth, amplified, and confirmed, by a considerate attention to the desires, the necessities, and the peculiar position, of these remarkable classes.

If their confidence be won—and won it may be by consistent kindness—they will listen to the word of advice, and act upon it; they will hail the spiritual, as well as the temporal, counsellor; and hymns of praise and prayer may be heard in the back slums of Whitechapel and St. Luke's, as fervent and as true—pos-

* "The Book and the Man,"—a most interesting work.

sibly more so — as in the Metropolitan Cathedral of St. Paul's.

Very enormous segments of our London population are now under the guidance and care of individual Missions; and it is to one of these, Mr. Orsman's in Golden Lane, to which the Author mainly directs the public attention.

The account of the rise, condition, and progress of these Missions, would be a deeply interesting and most curious chapter in the interior history of England. At present we can say no more of them than that they are some sixty or seventy in number; that tens of thousands, but for such efforts, would never be taught in the word of God, never hear the language of sympathy, or enjoy a helping hand. Their founders and conductors are called 'Self-constituted,' and 'In-truders' on the sacred office. For my own part, I love the text of our blessed Lord—'By their fruits ye shall know them.' And if supplication and thanksgiving, purity and peace, faith and assurance, in many hearts, be fruits according to the Gospel, these 'Intruders' require no other proof of their real and effective ordination.

To carry on the secular part of these operations after an alms-giving fashion, would be the ruin of the people; but the missionaries and writers, such as the Author of the present volume, advise and practice a very different course. The whole system proceeds on the trite and well-known rule, 'Aid those who aid themselves.'

Doubtless, in the various occupations of the working-sort, there are various methods of assistance, but Loan-funds are beneficial in them all. Petty sums so advanced, recover many, start many, and maintain many, in the career of a decent livelihood.

To insist on speedy and punctual repayment by small instalments, no interest being demanded; and on the co-responsibility of a security, gives to the whole an air of business, and preserves the right relations of debtor and creditor. The gratitude of the recipients is a sufficient proof of the moral results of these institutions.

I see our Author records the definition of a ' Coster,' as given by himself — ' A Coster,' said his informant, ' is a cove wot works werry 'ard for a werry poor livin'.' This is the definition of no end of small traders among the four millions of our amazing metropolis. Our object should be not so much to reduce the labour, as to make it remunerative. And here it is that a little opportune help enables these enterprising people to avail themselves of times, and secure markets and merchandize. And while they are quick and bold to labour for ' the meat that perisheth,' not a few of them, we are thankful to say, are ready to acknowledge that ' Man doth not live by bread alone, but by every word that proceedeth out of the mouth of God.'

SHAFTESBURY.

CASTLE WEMYSS,
    WEMYSS BAY,
  August 25th, 1873.

PART I.—LONDON.

I.

GOLDEN LANE.

I.

GOLDEN LANE.

ERSONS who have not seen something of the every-day life of Golden-lane and Whitecross-street, and the working of Mr. Orsman's mission—a valuable mission in that remarkable neighbourhood,—cannot say that they have really seen the great world of London. Passing along Old-street, the passenger comes suddenly upon the dingy entrance to the thoroughfares named, and if he have an eye to take in what is archæologically picturesque, he will surely find something in the close frowning streets to repay a passing inspection. There is always something about ancient roadways which, though not easily defined, seems to bid strangers linger, and learn what is there to be told about the past; and notwithstanding the abounding squalor and misery, we may learn many lessons also, such as may be turned to account in the present day.

'Moved by the highest considerations,' says Mr. Orsman, 'I was led, in April, 1861, to devote my leisure time, after office hours, to the hard task of evangelising the benighted costermongers, itinerant street - traders, and others, who herd together by thousands in the area circumscribed by Goswell-street, Old-street, Bunhill-row, and Chiswell-street. The district was in a terrible state of degradation, when, with the word of God in my hand and a bundle of " The British Workman " under my arm, I commenced the crusade against sin. In my first visits to these people I was compelled to witness the grossest immoralities, and to hear the foulest language from the lips of young and old. There were "Twopenny hopping-cribs," in which, stimulated by drink, the young of both sexes joined; drunken fights and robberies with violence were of daily occurrence. The sanitary condition of the district was equally bad. The alleys reeked with the foul refuse of fish and vegetables, and the open drains polluted the air, spreading disease far and wide.

'Notwithstanding we have lived to see a marvellous change for good come over the district in which we labour, there is much, very much yet to be done. Infidelity, with the notorious Bradlaugh as its leader, has its head-quarters in our midst; low beer-shops and public-houses are flauntingly attractive at almost every corner; the courts and alleys are still crowded with unhealthy hovels, and swarm with men, women, and children.

'Beyond Golden-lane, which is inhabited entirely by persons living daily from hand to mouth, the condition of the masses of St. Luke's, as of other districts in London, is a subject for very anxious thought. High wages and low morals; political liberty of the widest kind; thousands of working men of various trades banding themselves together for "strikes;" open and secret sceptical and republican clubs jointly springing up on every side; the spread of Jesuitical Ritualism; the growing profanation of the Lord's-day, and the utter indifference of the people to vital godliness, call for the most lively sympathy and earnest action on the part of every true Christian throughout the land.

' These masses *must* be leavened by the Gospel; but what are we among so many? " The harvest truly is plenteous, but the labourers are few; pray ye therefore the Lord of the harvest that He will send more labourers into His harvest."

'The Reports contain much interesting information on the various classes who earn precarious livelihoods, and sketches of coster-monger and itinerant street-trade life, as well as the method of our Evangelistic work among them, which has been, and is still carried on in entire dependence on God to supply all our needs through His children. No collector is employed, and all donations are promptly acknowledged in writing to the sender. The accounts are carefully kept and audited by well-qualified gentlemen, and the books are always open for the inspection of friends interested in our work. Many donors have personally visited us, as well as friends from America and the Continent, whom we are always glad to see.'

Here then is Golden-lane. Perhaps the district should be doubly interesting in the eyes of Christian philanthropists, because of its not being a thoroughly bad neighbourhood in the criminal sense. The densely-packed courts are not mere refuges for bad characters, as one might judge from appearances; for in a great part they are occupied by costermongers and street-sellers, or, as they would call themselves, general dealers. 'These costers are a hard-working, patient, enduring class, accustomed to making many shifts when times are 'quiet,' or when the commodities they deal in command prices in the open market which suit neither the coster's capital nor the pockets of his humble customers. Dr. Johnson defined ' cos-termonger' as 'a person who sells apples.' A more trustworthy authority on such a ques-tion — a citizen of Mr. Orsman's territory — summarily sets aside the lexicographer's inter-pretation as a popular error of the Georgian era. In fact, he declares 'a person who sells apples' to be 'all gammon,' and then con-siderately explains that a coster is 'a cove wot works werry 'ard for a werry poor livin', and is always a bein' hinterfered with, and blowed up, and moved hon, and fined, and sent to quod by the beaks and bobbies.' But if in this degenerate age this useful class are accustomed to hard work, hard fare, and hard usage, they are at least able to lay claim to a lineage ancient, if not proud. Thus we are told by one journalist, that 'the costermongers of Golden-lane and Whitecross-street are the direct descendants of the " costard-mongers " mentioned by Ben Jonson and his contemporaries, and of the street traders who, in after years, furnished such abundant material for the pencil of Hogarth. There are costermongers in Whitecross-street who can trace their descent in an almost unbroken line to the time when Golden-lane was lined with hedge-rows, beyond which were green fields and smiling gardens, amid which the sightless author of " Paradise Lost " loved to stroll, when staying at his residence in Barbican, close by. There exists a

3 *

curious resemblance in form and feature between the costermonger of St. Luke's and many of the street traders in Hogarth's pictures, for to this day the "costers" preserve many of their old characteristics, not the least marked being their intense dislike of the police, who have replaced the old "Charlies," a feeling which is duly reciprocated by the blue-coated representatives of the law. In olden time the costers who now throng Whitecross-street were spread over the City, and had stalls in Fore-street, Grub-street, Redcross-street, and other City thoroughfares, but as the value of City property increased, and the need for keeping the principal streets free from obstruction became more and more urgent, the costermongers and street traders were driven back step by step until they reached Whitecross-street, so that this part of London has become the metropolis for costermongerdom.'

The coster of London who succeeds at his

calling will often be found to possess a shrewd business head. He may not have mastered the arts of reading and writing; but, while perambulating the London markets, his quick eye readily fixes on whatever will turn his penny. When times are good — *i. e.*, when goods are cheap — it is his delight to attend Covent-garden, Spitalfields, or Billingsgate, rather late in the morning, and after the regular tradesmen are served, to clear away the remnants at a cheap rate. Thus it often happens that dealers who are obliged to purchase before a certain hour, find themselves in competition with sellers who are able to retail at a profit goods equal in quality to those in the shops, but at a reduced rate. The coster, however, is a good servant of the poor, and of the lower middle-class generally. He can live on smaller profits than the shopkeeper, and when a glut occurs in the market, he quickly distributes goods with which his more powerful rivals would not care to trouble themselves.

Golden - lane, then, is the metropolis of the nation of costers; and Mr. Orsman, the voluntary evangelist of the province, is a potentate whose mere word goes forth with more authority among the natives than the strongest official menaces. China - yard is, perhaps, the most famous rendezvous of the street-sellers, and our frontispiece represents the costermonger in his every day aspect. Very recently I passed some hours with Mr. Orsman and his chosen constituents, when I saw sufficient to verify the correctness of reports previously heard concerning the great evangelistic work in progress. It was Monday evening, and after seven o'clock the mission station began to show signs of life. Into one room persons of the costermongering type were passing to pay hard-won deposits into the penny bank, and the business transacted proved the existence of thrift and foresight among the poor, engendered by Christianity, such as was not known in Golden-lane a dozen years ago, and which the majority of our friends would not have supposed any agency could have awakened. Poor women came with their scanty savings, while many pence and small silver coins were brought by children. In one instance a man over seventy years of age was found making a provision against the time when he would be entirely laid aside by infirmity. As a supplement to the bank, 'The Emily Fund'* lends capital,

* Em'ly ain't a gal; Em'ly is the name of a fund at the Golden-lane Mission wot the wimmen an' gals borrers from. I thinks this is 'ow it cum'd about. Our President, the Earl, 'ad as good a wife as ever trod a pair o' shoes, an' wen she died, poor crittur, an' went tu 'even, the Earl, insted o' tryin' tu forget her, as a good menny does—he sez tu his sons an' dorters,—I forgets their names,—he sez, ' Supposin' we giv sum money tu the Water-cress sellers' Mishun, an' Mr. Orsman's Mishun, tu lend out without any interest tu the wimmen wots 'ard up tu bi stock with, an' call it

free of interest, to female street-sellers. This
charity is named after, and is established in
memory of, the late Countess of Shaftesbury;

the Em'ly Fund, arter Mrs. Shaftesbury.' An' a werry
good fund it is tu. It's 'elped nearly fifty pepel alreddy,
an' will 'elp hundreds if all pays back wot they borrers.
Sum on 'em sells wegitabels an' greenstuff; some sells
coke; sum, chumps o' wood; sum, creases ; sum, flowers ;
an' I sees ole Mary the 'erb 'ooman ez got suffink, an'
Jinny wot sells Cow-heels (the name of the alley were
I used tu hang out), an' sheep's trotters. This ez bin
one of the wust winters I ever seed, an' no mistake :
wot with coals at seven pounds for tuppens-ha'penny ;
an' meat an' all sorts o' things werry dear, most on us
ez 'ed tu part with our stock money tu bi grub with,
an' so our missuses cant go out as they used tu, cos
there's nothink tu go out with. But God is good, and
when He shuts up one door He opens another. On
cors there's them pepel wot lends a quid (a £1), from
Friday tu Sunday nite, wen yer pays it back with a bob
(1s.), for interest. If a chap borrers a £1 every week
for a year, he ez to pay £2 12s. interest for it. I likes
yer fund, cos ther's nothink tu pay for interest. I wishes
there wos a great many more Earls o' Shaftesbury tu
'elp us poor corsters wen we are doun on our luck : that's
the rite sort o' religun—tu 'elp them wot trise to 'elp
themselfs.—*Coster Jack in The Golden Lane Mission
Magazine.*

and is a valuable agency much appreciated by the poor women and girls for whose special benefit it was instituted. To linger in the ante-room after the bank business has closed, is to see divers eager applicants for this coveted boon, which effectively teaches the poor to help themselves.

But what chiefly concerns us to-night is not anything belonging to banks or charities; not even the devotional meeting in the large room, where fervently earnest prayers by poor women and others are offered, and some hymns are sweetly rendered — we have to attend a meeting of costers in one of the lower apartments of the mission house. This interesting assembly is composed of the members of 'The London Union of General Dealers,' who meet here this evening for the first time. The reason why the men have found their way into this hospitable shelter will need a word of explanation. Late in the autumn of last year the vestry of St. Luke's purposed issuing an edict forbidding the costermongering fraternity any longer to trade in Whitecross-street; and probably the vestry would have carried out its great idea had it not been for the timely advice and representations of Lord Shaftesbury and Mr. Orsman. It may be remembered that when news of the parish magnates having relented gained currency, the extravagantly - expressed joy of the poor people astonished many to whom the good things of life come too regularly for them always to remember their gratitude to the Giver. Out of the excitement of that time sprang the benefit and protection club referred to above. Many of the men would have liked to identify this club with the mission, had not circumstances fought against them. One of the principal promoters of the movement was a far-gone atheist, and, as a speaker explained, this gentleman gave his compeers distinctly to understand that 'he would 'ave nothink wotever to do with the business if the meetins wos 'eld at a misshun 'all.' Thus for the sake of securing the valued services of this enlightened coadjutor, the little society turned its back on Mr. Orsman's station, and took up its abode as a club at a public-house hard by. Evil consequences followed. The atheist and his employers soon disagreed, and not without reason, for he used them ill and served them badly. Thus, after having their books and general business plunged into a state of confusion, from which it will require both time and patience to extricate them, the deluded costers were glad to accept Mr. Orsman's offer to enjoy the use of a room every Tuesday night, free of all charges.

Entering the meeting with Mr. Orsman, I find a goodly number already gathered, and others arrive until the room is crowded. It is a costers' business meeting purely and simply.

Though no intoxicants of any kind are allowed
to enter, a conveniently situated cupboard is
seen to be amply furnished with ginger-beer,
lemonade, and cake; and these refreshments are
served out by a stout custodian as fast as the
gentlemen present choose to hand over the
reasonable charge of a penny for a bottle or a
slice respectively. As Mr. Orsman merely looks
in as a visitor, he takes no active part in the
proceedings; but his countenance and advice
are so eagerly sought and valued by the men,
that he cannot easily get away again. Before
the business meeting begins, a running conversation is kept up, the ruling genius among the
costers being a thick-set, cleanly-looking dealer,
who answers to the name of Wilkins. Wilkins
appears to wield a certain authority, besides
which he is a man who enjoys considerable
popularity among his order as a speaker in
public and as an adviser in general. When
Wilkins, distrusting his own judgment, requires

counsel's advice, he removes his hat, rises to his feet, and addresses Mr. Orsman. It is true that he lays no claim to the possession of oratorical gifts, and so exemplifies a humility which must be quite affecting to his more lowly neighbours; but as we are informed in significant tones, Mr. Wilkins can speak his mind when 'the shoe pinches.' As there is a general talk about barrows, Mr. Orsman takes the opportunity of explaining the working of the excellent club connected with the mission. It is an immense advantage to a street-dealer if he can command a vehicle of his own, and therefore it is now shown how the needful capital of seventy shillings may be saved. Seventy shillings did Mr. Orsman say? He must please remember that barrows, even, have 'gone up.' Nay, he is informed somewhat authoritatively by Wilkins, and by others who second that gentleman's affirmation, that, 'A good barrer now costs four pound, and from that to four pun' ten.'

There is one enviable individual present who has actually paid ' seven pound ' for his barrow; and the proud smile of self-appreciation, not to say of condescension, with which he communicates the fact, shows that the aristocracy of street-traders understand something of the respect due to themselves and to their position in life. The ' seven pound barrer ' has expensive appliances for carrying fire-wood, not required by ordinary traffickers.

' But, Wilkins, you are chairman of this meeting, take your place,' says Mr. Orsman, putting an end to minor discussions. The gentleman addressed now steps to the front, and, with a glass of ginger-beer on his right hand, proceeds to business. That Wilkins is a power among costers is self-evident. The company drink in his words as coming from one who, both by native ability and by acquired talents, is qualified to occupy the position of ' cheerman to this society.' In quite a straightforward manner, the difficulties into which the club has been plunged by its late atheistical secretary are explained, and Mr. Wilkins vents his indignation in a manner calculated to show that the laws against libel are not respected by his order. When anything hits exceptionally hard it is welcomed by vociferous acclamations, such as shake the house, and obliging the chairman to take breathing time, also allows of some attention being given to the ginger-beer on the right. Nor is the applause less deafening when anything pleasing is spoken, — as for example, when Mr. Wilkins proposes that 'the Herl' be requested to honour the society by becoming president, and that Mr. Orsman also honour them by becoming treasurer. But there is one sombre difficulty lagging in the back-ground, as yet not alluded to — a secretary is wanted! If the poor fellows crowding this room only possessed those master gifts with which secretaries are supposed to be endowed, how hotly would this office be competed for with its certain emoluments of threepence per quarter from each member. Alas! not one coster can aspire to the position. Situated thus, the only alternative is to confess defeat or ask Mr. Orsman to supply the deficiency, provided it be understood that the men will insist on the gentleman's accepting fees. In a few minutes, amid loud cheers, it is announced that a resident in the district, who will pay his salary back to the funds of the society, will serve the men as desired.

We now rise to leave a meeting which, on the whole, has been quite orderly, and the entire absence of improper expressions has told much in favour of the Christianising influence of the Golden-lane Mission. Not that there have been no obstreperous persons present to provoke cries of 'cheer, cheer,' until Mr. Wilkins necessarily exercised a chairman's authority; we merely say the proceedings were as orderly as most other meetings where numbers of men associate for business purposes. What also appeared striking was the unlimited authority wielded over the men by Mr. Orsman. It was the homage of real respect, paid by hard-working fellows, who, on the average, are probably as honest as traders of a higher class. Yes, their homage is paid to one whose life of voluntary self-sacrifice commands the admiration and gratitude even of those who may not be able to understand its spring.

In the mean time, places like Golden-lane and Whitecross-street, to be well understood, must be seen under different aspects. They must be seen on the Sabbath as well as on week-days. Like all other great centres of population, London is a city of contrasts, but the contrasts are perhaps more striking on Sunday morning than at another time. The quiet of rural lanes scarce surpasses the stillness of many streets around Cheapside when the Sabbath dawns. Alive with the hum and eager competition of commerce during the week, these places are as forsaken on Sundays as if a panic had seized the traffickers to occasion their precipitately retreating like an affrighted army. Emerge from these avenues of dormant warehouses, and step into one of the Sabbath markets, and how changed is the scene! It is as though the scattered builders of Babel, having reunited, were there in confusion of tongues disputing for mastery. Take places like Whitecross-street and Leather-lane, and, if you understand London life, you will see at a glance how much there is in a Sabbath market to attract and interest the lower classes. The street, with its confusion of voices and mud ankle-deep, is to the vulgar crowd a fair and a world in itself. What disgusts genteel visitors possesses fascinations for others less fastidious. You are a person of taste: so is the artisan or labourer in morning déshabillé yonder, though his taste may be coarser than yours. The market is a scene of life such as he thoroughly enjoys, provided the sky be clear and the wind be not too biting to hinder his standing at the street corner to smoke and gossip. Even small shopkeepers are persons honoured in a way by the class beneath them. Humble customers appreciate the opportunity of lingering over a bargain, or of chatting over the process of paying another instalment off the accumulating score. They would not attend the ordinary public worship of God were there no market, and they prefer the street to a confined, dirty home. They would not hear the Gospel at all were not the mission station open, and its agents abroad to seek for the people the good they will not seek for themselves.

In certain of these markets the stalls are packed closely together, and are heavily laden with vegetables, earthenware, toys, and other goods,, all of which are pressed upon public notice with eager looks and shrill cries. These Sunday fairs were formerly allowed to remain during the whole morning, but in Whitecross-street, as well as in other localities, a compromise has been arranged with threatening vestries, and a clearance has to be effected by eleven a.m.

But though vestries may oust poor costers, they can interfere little with the shops. These being less subject to the authority of Bumbledom, open wide their doors, and should it suit their convenience, they will employ a person to take up a position on the pavement whose natural gifts chiefly consist in a capacity for making unlimited noise. I have even met with a Sabbath auction in one notorious thorough-fare. ' Pass in, genelmen, jest a goin' to commence '— and the numbers who did pass in to the frouzy store showed that auctions possess charms for a class of loungers with whom time passes heavily before the taverns open at one o'clock. Yet all these are missionary subjects, and experience has proved that not a few may be gathered into the Gospel fold.

Yes, he who would know anything about the manners and customs of the London poor must see them in the Sunday market. How interested they become in mere trifles, such as the marking of a bird and the cost of a chisel. Cannot they be taught to show some interest in the Gospel? See, yonder is a man selling braces on the pavement, and a popular preacher might be proud while commanding an audience as attentive as the one gathered around that dealer. Those braces, now, are such palpable bargains, that the salesman seems to think he is justified in being patronising. He is not going to ask half-a-crown, not even eighteen-pence for a pair — the price is one shilling only. He does a trade, and doubtless pities those who, unimpressed by noise and argument, deny themselves a luxury by withholding their shilling.

A person even more successful, to judge by the crowd he attracted, was a hat salesman whom we have encountered. This genius, whose mouth was too large to show a gentle origin, and whose lungs were too powerful to warrant our approaching within a certain number of yards of his shop door, may have owed much of his popularity to a green hat with a purple rim with which he adorned his person, for the purpose of producing a picturesque effect. 'Take up the 'ats, genelmen, and judge the harticles for yerselves. If you don't buy, why there's no 'arm done, cos this 'ere ain't like a ware'ouse as yer goes in and then don't like to come out on again without buying nothink.' A crowd of curious men examine the hats, and half-crowns pass rather rapidly from the pockets of purchasers to the till of the seller. This trade is stimulated by the premium of a cigar with every hat sold. This, then, is the nature of the soil on which London evangelists labour for a harvest. *They* must work hard and patiently to gather a congregation. An interested crowd may be gathered in a few minutes by the shameless chicanery of petty traders.

If any one person is known better than another in the purlieus of Golden-lane, that individual is Lord Shaftesbury, or ' The Earl,' as the people invariably call him. He is quite an idol among the costers, and is reckoned one of their number. On the day that the Princess Louise was married, in June, 1871, the President of the Mission left the wedding party at Windsor to attend the annual festival of the dealers, when he was welcomed by a native, who, mounted on ' The Earl' barrow, made a characteristic speech. Lord Shaftesbury has been presented with several testimonials by his lowly friends, such as a photograph of costers selling in Whitecross-street, a gold pencil-case, and a bouquet for the ladies at home. When the late Countess lay in her last illness, it is well known how the converts of Mr. Orsman's Mission sent up to heaven their earnest prayers for her ladyship's speedy recovery.

'The huge wave of sorrow as it rolls over the great city deposits its dark sediment here,' says our evangelist in reference to his district. His words may be readily credited when we consider that twenty thousand persons are huddled together within the radius of a furlong from the mission station. Of these, ' thirty per cent. are costermongers and itinerant street-traders; twenty per cent. are labourers and poor women, who live by washing, charing, and needlework; thirty per cent. are either paupers or persons of doubtful occupation; and the remaining twenty per cent. are industriously wearing out their lives in the attempt to earn a livelihood at the following occupations :—arti-ficial-flower makers; brace-sewing at twopence per dozen pairs; toy-makers, wood-choppers, and crossing-sweepers; gutter-searchers for cigar-ends; bone pickers, and dust-bin searchers for doctors' bottles, which, when washed, are sold to chemists at one shilling and ninepence per gross. Also fusee, sweetstuff, and herb sellers, dealers in old clothes, and sorters of the clearings of warehouses,' &c.

To commence work among this mass of wretchedness and heathenism with a stock-in-trade of a Bible and a bundle of tracts, revealed the existence of faith and moral courage such as few can rejoice in possessing. Answers to prayer were on the wing, however, and rewards also, since one convert's confession like the following—and many such came forward—would repay for a large outlay of persevering toil. '"Now mates, yer thinks yer sees Bill Wilkins, don't yer? An' so yer do, but not the same man yer used to see, an' I'll tell yer how it is. Yer knows how I used to go to Hornsey with my nets a bird-catching every Sunday, an' how I used to come home drunk and 'ave a row with the missus. Well, about three year ago I was comin' home a swearin' to myself 'cos I couldn't get my usual beer as they sez as how I wasn't a bony-fidy traveller. Well, I sees the people a-comin' out of church, an' I envied 'em; then I listens to a street-preacher who offered me a tract. Sez I, ' No use to me, guv'nor.' ' Why ?' ' 'Cos I can't read.' ' Then come to our mission-hall this evening,' says he." He then described his first visit to the mission, and how " that ere party I sees in the mornin' takes me right afore all the people to a seat close agin the preacher, an' I wished I hadn't 'ave gone," &c. The words, " God so loved the world," &c., touched his heart, and he went home a wiser and a better man. He suffered much pecuniary loss in his trade, and although much persecuted at home and elsewhere, he was consistent and useful in his life, and he died, as he had lived, rich in faith.'

After conversion these men can detail their

experience, and can define the Gospel before their own companions in language clear and forcible, as well as affecting. Listen to one of Mr. Orsman's converts, as he addresses a crowded meeting of costers :—

'The main p'int of this meeting, my friends, as I consider it, is to p'int ye to the Lamb of God. "Who hath believed our report? and to whom hath the arm of the Lord been revealed?" Bless the Lord it has been revealed to me. Ye all know what I were, and I 'ave to tell yer what I am. One text of Scripter has stuck by me — "God so loved the world, that he gave His only-begotten Son, that whosoever"—mind, *whosoever*, that takes all in, and leaves none out — "believeth in Him should not perish, but have everlasting life." One day, afore I were converted, when I were in liquor, I said to a policeman that I'd knock his brains out. He took me up. As we was going along to the magistrate next morning, I says to him, "Now, Mr. X., what do you think I should do?" "Why," said he, "plead guilty." So when I was taken afore the magistrate, he axed me what I had to say. I said, "*Guilty*, my lord, and I'm very sorry for what I've done." Then he fined me half-a-crown, or be locked up. But I was skinned out. Ye all know, my friends, what it is to be skinned out. So I was locked up. But presently the turnkey who locked me up came back, turned the key t'other way, opened the door, and told me to go out. Somebody had paid the fine for me; and when I got outside the walls, a man on the other side of the street made a sign to me wi' his finger to come to him; and when I went he put three shillings and sixpence into my hand, so that I had something to go on wi'. Now, my friends, Jesus Christ opens the door of our prison for us, sets us free, and gives us everlasting life to begin wi'. Ain't this wonderful! And He invites ye all to trust Him.'

In another instance, a child in the school became the means of her parents' conversion. Her sister having died of an infectious disease, this little one was sent from home, to be away until after the funeral. Unknown to her friends, however, she returned, and was found kneeling in prayer beside her sister's coffin — 'I am one of Thy lambs, and so I want to leave this wicked world.' The mother, moved to tears, may have foreseen the sequel — the little creature soon sickened, and then died, singing one of the hymns she had learned in her class.

Here are other examples of work, selected from many more, and given in Mr. Orsman's own words :—

' Men and women, ungodly in their lives, when dying have sent for us, and in some cases we have witnessed terrible scenes. Here is a specimen : — A widow with four children, of the respective ages of thirteen, eleven, eight, and five years, and a married daughter and her husband, lived in a back room ten feet square, and for which he paid two shillings and ninepence weekly. When visited, all were ill with the fever. The mother and child died shortly afterwards. The room was filthy and desolate : it contained only a broken table, four chairs tied up with pieces of string, and a broken looking-glass. The bodies of the deceased were like the room, and we had even to supply coverings to bury them in. One evening we were sent for to visit the father of some of our Band of Hope scholars. He was dying of bronchitis, struck down in the prime of life. In the same room lay his wife, in a delirious fever. The poor man was unconscious, and all efforts to rouse him seemed fruitless. His aged mother and many other relatives were weeping round the bed, hoping that he might at last rally sufficiently to hear the sweet message of the Gospel, and to avow his faith in Jesus. Just as we were about to leave, it was suggested that we should sing some hymns that he loved to hear his children sing. We sang softly, the hymn, " Just as I am ;" but he seemed to hear not until we sang—

" Rock of Ages, cleft for me."

And when we reached the last verse, his lips moved— his eyes lighted up with unearthly fire, and he sang audibly the last two lines. He died that night, and we trust he is now singing the everlasting song. A young lad recently caught the fever, and died, after two days' illness, in the hospital. Singularly enough, on the previous Sunday he had prayed in the Bible-class—for the first time in public. For three months previously he had been a true Christian. His sudden death has been the means of leading his parents to the house of God. A year ago we were sent for to visit a young married woman of respectable family, who was nearly frantic with terror at the prospect of death. She had caught cold at a ball, and rapid consumption had set in. When we first saw her, the doctor had just given her up. We read, prayed, and talked with her many times after that, and we had the delight of hearing her testimony to the love of Christ. She is gone to be with the angels, and her father and family now regularly attend the mission.'

Many converts in this district, which a few years ago was not over safe to pass through after nightfall, can tell of strange experience; and when one can be persuaded to become an autobiographer, a striking life-story, harrowing in its details, may possibly be the result. One of Mr. Orsman's converts thus writes about herself:—

'In one of the London model lodging-houses, about

seven years ago, there might have been seen a family which consisted of the following members: a man nearly forty-five years of age, four children, whose ages ranged from four to ten, an infant a week old, and a young woman nineteen years of age. It was plain, even to a casual observer, that an improper familiarity existed between the man and young woman. The infant of which we have spoken was hers, and although it had been born such a short time, the mother exhibited a black eye and swollen jaw. The man was a widower; his wife had died a year before, leaving an infant three weeks old. During her illness she had been carefully nursed by the young woman already mentioned, and who was betrothed to the dying woman's son. Before she died she had begged her kind nurse to look after her children when she was gone, a sacred duty which was willingly accepted. Not long after the death of his wife the husband sought an opportunity to seduce the young woman. In an evil hour, under the influence of strong drink, her ruin was effected. Her sweetheart, when he discovered it, enlisted for a soldier; and thus we find this young woman hiding her shame and burying her days with this man, passing off before the world as his wife. The aspect of the room bespoke the most abject poverty; miserable food and scanty clothing were telling on the inmates' health. A year after this a change took place. Actuated by more evil motives than those which prompted him to seduce and ill use a young woman, he deserted her on the 3rd of June, leaving his four children and her own little one to battle with a world to which she had hitherto been a stranger. For two days the poor girl was in a state of mind bordering on distraction. She determined to send his four children to a relative, sell the miserable home to a broker, and throw herself and child on the mercy of friends, from whom, however, she expected but little. For six weeks they supported her, but, with the exception of blows, she led a worse life than when co-habiting with the man. Treated with contempt, and working like a slave, she thought of suicide. Sugar of lead was obtained, but she over-dosed herself, and the hand of God prevented her from rushing unprepared into the presence of her Judge. Her reason left her; she was removed to the insane ward of the workhouse, and when, after three weeks, it pleased God to restore her senses, she found out the dreadful truth that she was again likely to become a mother. She resolved to leave the workhouse and seek her living in the world. She took her babe, and without a penny went forth. For two days they tasted nothing but the scanty allowance from the casual wards of Marylebone and St. Pancras, where she slept at night, after walking the streets all day. She saw her folly in leaving the workhouse, and again entered it. Her baby was taken from her and placed in the nursery, among children infected with measles, itch, whooping-cough, &c. The baby was pining away, and the mother could plainly see that it was fretting itself to death. She could not bear the thought of her child thus dying, and she obtained her discharge from the house. Once more she was in the streets, homeless and friendless. It was a pitiful sight; a dying babe in a sinful, but withal a true-hearted mother's arms. For days she wandered about and slept in the tramp-sheds at night. This state of things told upon her health. One night, while sleeping in the casual ward of the West London Union, she was taken so ill that the superintendent sent to her own parish for a messenger to take her there. Her baby now was dying, and it pleased God in His mercy to take it home to Himself. She saw the babe buried, and once more threw herself on the world, but not for long, for the next night she was taken to the workhouse again, and again became the mother of a boy. At the end of four months she obtained her discharge and five shillings from the Board. She made her way to the place where she first fell in Golden-lane, and entered one of the tramps' kitchens.

The most devilish forms of immorality and vice prevailed there, and the scenes which she nightly witnessed were so repulsive that she accepted the proposal of a once fellow-pauper, whom she met in the street, to go and live with her. She soon discovered that her benefactress was both a prostitute and a thief, and her spirit revolted at living on such ill-gotten gains. She left this abode of infamy, and for a few days wandered about the streets, and slept on door-steps and under railway arches, till she was well nigh starving. Again she appealed to the Board of Guardians for relief without going into the house. She was granted five shillings; and now, free from evil companions, she entered a common lodging-house. One night an inmate apprised her of a plot, by some rough fellows, to enter her bedroom and make an onslaught on her defenceless condition. In a state

of mind bordering on madness she left the house, and,
thinking herself too vile to seek a refuge in prayer to
God, she again meditated suicide. She dare not drown
her infant, and could not find it in her heart to leave it
to the mercy of the world: thus she was spared from
committing the dreadful deed. Oh, the reward of crime!
Here was a young woman hungry and cold, for she had
to go without food to pay for the bed from which she
had to fly, an infant vainly trying to draw support from
a milkless breast, and without a friend in the world.
Where could she go? what could she do? The Friend
of the friendless looked down upon her, and again
directed her steps to the workhouse. She repined at
her lot, but the awful fact stared her in the face that
she had disregarded the example and deathbed advice
of her Christian father, and that she had departed from
the paths of virtue. Another trial awaited her: the
baby was taken ill and died. She rebelled against the
All-wise providence, for she could not see His wisdom
in taking her child to a better home. She sought for
means to destroy her life; but poison was not obtainable,
the knives were out of her reach, and the windows so
constructed that she could not throw herself out of them.
The kind-hearted matron one morning told her that
she had obtained a situation for her, and would give her
necessary clothing. Though she rejoiced in heart, there
were no words of thankfulness to the Almighty: no, she
thought her fortune was turning, and that though she
had sinned, she had lived a moral life hitherto, which
amply compensated for the sin of the past.'

The writer suddenly stops in her history where the best part requires to be told. She was taken to the missionary meeting by some Christian people, who in the model lodging-house had frequently interfered to shield her from the violence of a drunken paramour. At the meeting she formed good resolutions, which were soon forgotten. There she affected to refuse religion, by turning sacred things into ridicule, until she was turned back from this dangerous path. 'At last the Spirit of God touched her heart,' says Mr. Orsman; 'and a few Sundays ago, after I had spoken earnestly from the words, "How can these things be?" she came into the inquirers' meeting, broken down in spirit, weeping over her sins, and inconsolable. Earnest prayers were offered, and that night many hearts thanked God for what they had seen and heard. Shortly after she began to realise the power of a Saviour's love, and she is now humbly confessing Him in her daily life.' This young woman is now the valued matron of a public institution in America.

In regard to the regular preaching of the Gospel which takes place at the mission-house, a member of the Society of Friends, who once attended, remarks,—' The worship was very simple — a hymn — the Bible read and familiarly illustrated and expounded — prayer, in which we were asked to engage—a simple, well-arranged, clear, and educated sermon — a sermon which encouraged us personally. City life sharpens the apprehensions of the classes who live by their wits, and a clear line of thought and apt illustration seems to be well understood. The character of the address would have been listened to with respect and attention from any congregation. It is noteworthy that a period of silent prayer forms part of the proceedings, and the congregation are asked to pray, each for what they most need. Our attention was specially called to an important fact, that this is not merely a " preaching place." The audience is *not drawn together by any prospect of any temporal gain;* in fact, not a few have had to suffer, not only persecution but pecuniary loss, in consequence of their religious views.'

During the winter months the children's dinner is immensely popular. This was once visited by the correspondent of *The Daily Telegraph, e.g. :—*

'And, at the stroke of one o'clock, here they come trooping in, their young eyes twinkling in blissful expectancy as their young noses sniff the savoury stew seething in the cauldron below, and just done. I have not yet seen the cauldron. As they come swarming in, their tiny ill-shod feet and their uncovered arms and legs blue with cold, faster and thicker yet, till the doorway bids fair to be blocked up, and there is still a mob behind, I have misgivings as to my friend's declaration that there will be enough for all and to spare. And what an awful thing it would be if, say, only a dozen of these poor narrow-chested mites of things, who passed last night in a delicious dream of Irish stew, who smacked their lips over the breakfast slice of dry bread flavoured with the promise of it, should be sent empty away! I do not believe that they would survive the shock. They would faint and fall, still clutching the basin that was now a mockery and a snare: they would go mad and run amuck among their more fortunate stew-consuming brethren. Here they come, each one bringing his or her "dinner things." I wish the reader could see the choice collection! Handleless jugs, milk-cans, baking dishes, sauce tureens, small-sized tin saucepans, publicans' beer cans, tin washing bowls — anything. They come of all ages, from the sturdy street boy of ten to the tiny six-months-old baby in arms. There were scores of babies under two years old, brought by their sisters and brothers.'

Boys who come to dine in this fashion must come as becomingly attired as means will permit; hence the origin of the boys' sewing class. 'The use of that potent little weapon of civilisation, the needle, is not particularly well-known to many of the mothers of the neighbourhood,' says Mr. Orsman. 'There are many boys whose mothers are dead, or so habitually dead drunk, that their conveyance to the cemetery would be little loss from a domestic point of view. So,

some time ago, it was proposed to the young-
sters that if they had a mind to patch up their
rags a bit, patch-pieces would be found, and a
good-natured matron would show them the way
to stitch. The proposition was agreed to with
alacrity, and is still in high favour. The
"class," through the limited accommodation,
is restricted to thirty; and as in no case are
the boys found to be in possession of a spare
garment of the sort that so sorely needs repair,
it is a strictly private class, to which nobody is
admitted except on business. Any boy guilty
of "larking," or in any way disturbing the
sober propriety so essential to the existence of
the class, is instantly banished; and, to the
credit of the poor little ragged tailors, it is said
that such expulsions are rare. It is, perhaps,
only natural that the care and perplexity attending the stitching together of rags that will
scarcely bear the weight of a needle, should at
times incline the operators to meditate on the

advantage of being altogether independent of artificial covering. "Wouldn't it be fine to do without altogether, Jack!" I heard an enthusiastic youth of eight remarking to his friend. "Couldn't you get lots of browns from the coves on the homblibustes! They allers pitches at yer when your trowsis is tore. They'd pitch more if you give 'em more to pitch at, I'll be bound." "Ah!" rejoined the other, "so they might; but where'd you put the browns wot they pitched yer, if yer didn't have no pockets on?" An argument that effectually silenced the young philosopher, and reconciled him to his job of adapting the sleeves of his father's old jacket as legs to the still trustworthy "upper part" of his corduroys.'

I must not omit to state that Golden-lane has its annual holiday, and I will here introduce a description of the last summer excursion, which I specially prepared for a London newspaper.

'GOLDEN-LANE IN THE COUNTRY.

'" Golden-lane ain't dead yet," remarked an elderly dame on the morning of Wednesday, the 13th instant, who, besides being in morning *deshabille*, carried a jug with which she would pound the back of a neighbour if provoked to do so by a challenge of holiday wit. Boys and girls in the mission-house were cheering vociferously, while a crowd which rendered the narrow roadway well-nigh impassable showed that some exceptionally stirring occurrence was attracting the populace from the network of courts and alleys which constitutes the neighbourhood. The now well-known "124" was being besieged by a strong force of good-humoured assailants, who in many instances were also vainly clamouring for tickets. Then the banners and strains of holiday music told all strangers that Mr. Orsman's day and Sunday-school children, Bible-classes, and other friends, were about to depart on their annual excursion.

'It might well be an exciting time, when nearly eight hundred passengers, young and full grown, who rarely see the fields, realised the fact that a special train was even then being put in readiness to give them "a day in the country," at the People's Gardens, Willesden. The school classes were taken free, while outsiders—and hundreds of these were necessarily left behind—were charged sums varying from ninepence to one shilling and threepence, the tickets including railway fare and "a good tea." The costermongers'

renowned haunt was thus altogether *en fête*, business
being apparently entirely suspended while the pro-
cession formed, and, "preceded by the band," according
to the programme, marched in triumph to Broad-street
Station. The company was quite of a motley kind.
There were children of all sizes, as well as adults of
all ages, and on landing at Willesden, after half-an-
hour's pleasant run, their sudden invasion of the lanes
not a little astonished the good natives of the neighbourhood who were not in Mr. Orsman's secret.

'The People's Gardens are a new institution, being
enclosed from the Old Oak Common. Embracing a
wide area, a portion of the land is laid out in flower
beds, croquet lawns, and bowling greens, besides which
there are refreshment buildings, and an immense plat-
form. On arriving here at noon, the visitors understand that they are to begin the day's pleasure by
promenading the gardens, by shaking hands with everybody, and by inspecting what there is curious to see
in the panorama and menagerie. But Golden-lane
holiday-makers are able to do little in following a
programme until they have dined; and, as the large
company have for the most part furnished themselves with a picnic dinner, they are seen here, there,
and everywhere, dining on viands varying in quality
and quantity, and which sadly enough in some instances speak of the necessitous condition of the poor
people.

'It was agreeable to find that Mr. Orsman's notions
of what should characterise a day's outing were of

the right kind. It is surely a mistake on the part
of certain good people when they attempt to turn a
holiday excursion into a religious revival service; and
some who have done so do more than they would like
being accredited with 'in creating a distaste for religion
among those who are willing enough to attend Gospel
services at the right time and place. The earnest
evangelist strives to live above even the suspicion of
cant, and Mr. Orsman provides a holiday programme
which costers, their wives and offspring, can really
appreciate, while none of them doubt his zeal in the
work of evangelisation. After dinner the girls, first
the big ones and then the little ones, run and skip
for prizes, and wonderful to behold is the distribution
which follows of work-boxes, frocks, books, and even
lockets. A like liberality is manifested on behalf of
the boys. The strong lads run "three-legged" and
"wheelbarrow" races, jump in sacks, and in various
ways manage to create as much merriment as many
of the spectators are able to bear, until the bell an-
nounces tea. Later in the day the members of the
Bible-class also enter the lists as competitors for
prizes, and even costers' wives eagerly embrace opportunities of winning articles valuable in daily life, such
as teapots, stays, and other covetable things.

'Next on our programme comes the tea. The
children are to be served first; and truly the eagerness of the excitable little creatures over this feast
of the year is at once interesting and painful. As
a matter of propriety, bread-and-butter must be put

forward as a beginning; but " Shall we 'ave any cake, sir? Shall we 'ave any cake?" is asked in quick, impatient tones, again. and again: and the eyes of the questioners repeat the query — "Cake?" Yes, there it comes, and not on plates either, but piled up on capacious trays in a thoroughly liberal style; and that cheer after cheer should shake the large building in honour of currant cake is not at all surprising to those who are acquainted with the liking which Golden-laners entertain for the *entremets* of life. The second tea, provided for the adults, is a no less characteristic scene; and the consumptive powers of the large company unmistakably perplex and astonish the contractor at the head of the commissariat department. The loaves, the butter, and the plates of cake with which the tables were too scantily furnished are cleared as if in a twinkling; and the demand for a further supply comes forth in a Babel of shouts, perhaps the reverse of polite, and in a rattling of crockery ominously suggestive to the uninitiated of a breach of the peace. But "All's well that ends well;" and now follow the evening entertainments.

'Were not our space so limited, much more could be said about this remarkable "day in the country;" about the garden party, the fire-balloons, the fireworks, and other novelties on which Golden-lane still looks with favour. If anything could be read in the faces of the costers and their families, surely it was regret that such a season should come to an end at all. Nor was the return home at evening less triumphant than the coming out in the morning. At Broad-street Station another crowd awaited the return of the special train; and, in the mean time, Golden-lane itself was actually illuminated by several enthusiastic tradesmen of the vicinity, who provided coloured fire and other lights. Thus ended a day long to be remembered even by the genteel visitors who joined the excursion. What shall be said of the immense influence wielded by one man and his assistants over one of the poorest districts? Does it not speak more for the power of the Bible and of prayer than aught which so-called scientific objectors can advance against them? What is still more encouraging, Mr. Orsman has proved that there exists a wonderful readiness among the poor to receive the Gospel, when that Gospel is carried to them by those who understand its power.'

It must occasion Mr. Orsman no little joyful satisfaction when he looks around on the results of his toil. He can point to hundreds of persons who though once wallowing in profligacy are now adorning the Gospel. Numbers of his converts have emigrated, to become examples of Christian uprightness in foreign climes. Not a few whom he has been instrumental in raising socially, as well as spiritually, by the grand

ameliorating power of religion, are now occupying honourable positions in life. Some of
the rescued youths have entered the Civil Service, others are Sabbath-school teachers, while
a few are ministers of the Gospel.

Only completely to summarise the work accomplished in Golden-lane during one year
would be no easy task. First, the Gospel is
faithfully preached at the mission-house, where
also Bible-classes and inquirers' meetings are
held. There are special services for children,
a Sabbath-school served by teachers who are
converts of the Mission, and a free day-school,
in which we are told 'the best lesson-book is
the Bible.' Between four and five thousand
dinners are given away each winter to famish-
ing children. Then the scholars are taken
into the country for an excursion every year,
and 'the summer outing is looked forward
to as *the* event of the year by these poor
little ragged ones. . . . As the time draws

nigh they grow so nervous with excitement,
that it is very hard to restrain them.' Tea
and cake, followed by lectures and dissolv-
ing views, are occasional treats provided for
the adults of the neighbourhood; and of the
value of such entertainments we need har-
bour no doubts, since one woman testified when
dying, ' That picter o' the woman clingin' to
the cross, with the roarin' waves all around,
made me understand that beautiful hymn,—
" Simply to Thy cross I cling," an' now I know
He WILL save me.' Nor must we overlook the
soup-kitchen, the clothing and barrow clubs,
the ' Emily ' Fund, the visitation of the sick,
the mothers' sewing club, and the maternity
society. The boon conferred by this last is best
known to those who enter a room all but bare,
to carry with them comforts and necessary
clothing for some prostrate sufferer who has
scarce bed or covering to comfort her during
nature's trial.

In his great work Mr. Orsman has enlisted the gratitude and sympathy of the Church at large. While empty city churches are thickly scattered around his district, to serve no higher purpose than that of providing comfortable stipends for scholarly incumbents, or of interesting curious archæologists, this volunteer in Christ's service has stormed the very castle-keep of London heathenism, and to the surprise of his friends has successfully planted the Gospel standard on ground from which many have turned aside with a shudder as from a God-forsaken field. May his life long be spared to win yet greater trophies, and may all needful pecuniary support be offered by those who, possessing wealth, have learned to become cheerful givers to Him who gave Himself for them. In fine, may the new mission-building —as yet only ' one of the hopes of the future ' —soon be an accomplished fact; and may it testify to another generation of the holy courage and perseverance of a man whom posterity will remember and honour as the Apostle of Golden-lane.

The frontispiece appears by permission of the proprietors of *The Graphic;* and some persons may wish to know that Mr. Orsman's address is 75, Oakley-road, Islington.

NOTE BY MR. SPURGEON.—We know of no evangelistic work in London so wisely conducted and permanently useful as that which was inaugurated by Mr. Orsman, and has been carried on by him for so many years. Our beloved friend has always rejoiced in being connected with the Tabernacle, though he has not been dependent in any degree upon us for funds. Our heart rejoices at every remembrance of him. He is one of that honourable body of men who are not chargeable unto the churches, but abide in their callings and preach the Gospel freely. Only by labourers of this class can our back slums be reached. Hard by the very centre of infidelity, our brother exhibits a practical Christianity, and he ought to have the sympathy of all believers in so doing, a sympathy not of words only, but shown in pecuniary help towards the building he requires.

II.

THE TAVERNS OF PADDINGTON.

6 *

THE TAVERNS OF PADDINGTON.

NOT until a comparatively recent date have the aggressive forces of Christianity ventured on disputing the ground with the enemy by seeking trophies of victory in public-houses. Viewed from any standpoint the public-house mission is a daring innovation. When first proposed some years ago, the scheme appeared to be novel, and even Utopian; so that while ordinary people were disposed to smile derisively at the broaching of such an idea, many friends of missions and true helpers of the poor doubted the expediency of carrying Gospel pearls into places where they would probably be trampled under foot. These happily groundless fears may in part have arisen from popular misapprehen'sion as to the true nature of public-houses, and also of the sentiments of those who conduct them; for as regards this department of knowledge, the majority of easy-going people are likely to be in a condition of complete ignorance.

Public-houses differ very widely in character, and only in a few exceptional instances are they worthy of being denounced as altogether bad; while not a few are as respectably conducted as the nature of taverns will allow, closing on Sundays, and discouraging excess by every means. The characters of the landlords differ as widely as their houses. Unworthy characters are found among them, as they may be found among all other classes of tradesmen; but happily, numbers of men with sterling traits of character are found in the publican ranks.* Then why should not the Gospel be carried into taverns as well as into squalid courts and alleys ? As places of public resort, taverns would seem to be just the very places where those characters may be encountered whom the City Mission seeks to reclaim. If religion be out of place in a public-house, there must be something radically wrong somewhere; and to reiterate, as some are in the habit of doing, this popular opinion, is to condemn an influential trading community in a very sweeping manner, even though the opinion may come from persons who as nominal Christians see no harm in the calling of the licensed victualler. To raise objections on the ground of the two things being opposed to each other, is simply to asso-

* NOTE BY MR. SPURGEON.—We do not hold ourselves responsible for the way in which Mr. Pike puts the matter. We would not join in condemnatory sentences; but, for all that, the evils of the trade are incalculable.

ciate public-houses with what is bad, and with what is bad alone.*

It is believed that no class of tradesmen more readily listen to Christian advice than publicans. They are also both sensitive and hospitable, and were not their profession too often stigmatised as altogether bad by certain people, one obstacle to a reformation would be removed. As some, however, still persist in associating the public-house trade with depravity alone, Mr. Landlord may too often prefer leaving religion untouched, and so avoid being classed among hypocrites by the unthinkingly severe. Yet strange as the anomaly may perhaps appear, there are Christians even among publicans. Here is one, for instance, who professes religion, closes on Sundays, and

* NOTE BY MR. SPURGEON. — But a common public-house is not the place in which a person of such character would choose to live. The evils of the trade could not be endured by such: if they stayed in it they would be under daily trial.

subscribes to the funds of the London City Mission. There is another who speaks a good word for the tracts whenever they are distributed in his bar, while his daughter is a successful Sunday-school teacher. Yet another is met with who so strongly advocates 'fair-play,' that he desires to be allowed to pay for the literature given away in his house for philanthropic purposes. So far are publicans from being advocates of Sunday labour, that many, perhaps the majority who superintend their own trade, would welcome an agitation which would secure them their portion of weekly rest. On this head, my friend the missionary, whose work I am about to describe, thus testifies:—'The publicans, as a body, are not unconscious of the evils of their trade. They groan under the present state of things. Their desire to have the Sunday as a day of rest is general; and to secure this great boon and right for themselves, their families, and their assistants, they would gladly submit to some pecuniary loss. Many public-houses, however, are in the hands of capitalists, who employ active barmen and showy barmaids to serve and do the laborious part of the work. The unseen but powerful capitalists are the persons most opposed to any movement to secure a relaxation in the hours of business, especially on the Lord's-day. The legislature and the press are not willing to view the whole subject as affecting the publicans primarily, and, through them, their customers. Reform in this direction is further off, I fear, than it was a year since. All depends now on the efforts of private individuals and evangelical societies.' My friend ranks high in the favour of certain landlords, as, indeed, he ought to do; and the fact of his being so seldom interfered with in a somewhat obtrusive work, speaks something for the genial nature of publicans in general.

Feeling considerable interest in the work of tavern visitation for evangelistic purposes, I some time ago cultivated the acquaintance of a missionary in Marylebone, and gave to the public the fruits of a brief study of his operations.* Having since become acquainted with another missionary in Paddington, I now purpose detailing something of what he has also effected in the good cause.

From what many of us know of City Mission work, we shall, perhaps, suppose that the public-house visitor must be a picked man— a man in some respects a head and shoulders above his compeers. Such as are partially illiterate may become excellent workmen in ordinary districts, and many such could be named whose labours are evidently much owned of God. He, however, whose beat includes a

* See the chapter entitled 'Sunday Night in the Taverns,' in 'The Romance of the Streets.' (Hodder and Stoughton.)

large number of taverns, must not only have tact and kindliness, but also a large amount of information, both Biblical and secular: indeed, it would be difficult to name any literary accomplishment which such a man is not able to utilise. It is indispensable that he be a ready textuary, that he be acquainted with the ordinary infidel arguments against the Gospel, and be possessed of ready wit. He must also be one who is not easily ruffled in temper, while he must have an eye to perceive and a hand to seize opportunities as they occur. An agreeable testimony is offered when it is said that neither of the public-house visitors already named betrayed symptoms of falling short of the standard described.

Being no stranger to the efforts now put forth in public-houses, I felt curious to look yet further into the working of this remarkable agency. I therefore arranged to meet the missionary who has charge of the Paddington district, the time being a fine Saturday evening in August. Though you may never have met him before, you can readily detect the City Missionary, and he will tell you himself that it is impossible for persons of his profession to conceal their calling. It was not long ere my friend involuntarily convinced me of his peculiar fitness for his chosen work, for he seemed fully aware that to succeed in anything one must have a liking for the work undertaken. His circuit embraces four hundred houses of call; formerly a thousand houses were included in the area, and out of that large number not more than half-a-dozen landlords have offered any opposition to his aggressive operations. Estimated at its best, this is necessarily an arduous and a difficult calling, and fortunate is the missionary when his labours are encouraged by the advice and kindly assistance of some sympathising superintendent. Such

exactly is my friend's felicity. Not only has
each publican in Paddington been gratuitously
supplied with 'Prayers for a Week,' each has
also accepted a copy of the New Testament,
all being the gift of Mr. Ellis, Barrister-at-
law. Besides such extraordinary donations
of a more expensive kind, the distribution of
tracts and other publications regularly proceeds; two thousand tracts, and two hundred
and fifty copies of religious periodicals, being
the allowance received monthly from the committee of the London City Mission. While
it is not easy to estimate the influence which
one devoted man may thus be able to exercise, the fact speaks for itself when houses
here and there are found closed on the Sabbath, in deference to the evangelist's advice;
or when donations to good objects are made
in return for benefit received. An instance
has occurred in which a publican willingly
suffered a loss of eight hundred pounds a

year in his receipts through closing on Sundays. There are comparatively few landlords who do not appreciate what is being done for themselves and their customers. Sometimes, when a member of the trade is laid aside, or when any person in whom they feel extra interest falls sick, landlords will do their best to supply them with Christian instruction and consolation by acquainting the missionary.

Walking with my companion from the Bishop's-road station, the streets are found to wear that busy aspect supposed so well to harmonise with the last night of the week, though the quietness of preparation for the Sabbath would to our mind be far more appropriate. One looks into one, and then another, of the taverns of the larger order, thickly studding this 'good drinking neighbourhood,' and can only account for the lavish expenditure of substantial architecture and decoration by remembering how large a proportion of the wages of certain persons goes in drink. The field is indeed white unto the harvest, and I am glad to find that my companion considers himself well adapted for the work he has undertaken, seeing he has been acquainted from childhood with the manners and customs of licensed victuallers. He confesses to having been born in a public-house, and while the bar constituted the first infant-school he attended, the duly gilded announcement, 'Truman, Hanbury, Buxton, and Company's Entire,' was the first complete sentence in English with which his opening mind was enriched. That the son of a publican should desire to promote the publicans' benefit, and should thus become an active witness for Christianity among the class to which his father belonged, some will think sufficiently strange. A more striking anomaly is found in the fact that my friend's family were succeeded in the public-house by a teetotaller, and one who remained such until death. The anomaly-hunter will find wares ready-made to his hand in bars, and in scenes behind the bars.

We are now out on a special mission, and my companion, who does not usually visit on Saturday evenings, but has made this an extraordinary occasion, is equipped for service with a bundle of tracts in one pocket, a Bible in the other, and a black leather case which encloses 'The Cottager,' 'The Sunday at Home,' and 'The British Workman,' all to be distributed among tavern proprietors and their servants. We now come up to a large corner establishment or restaurant, where two waiters loitering at the side-door are soon in our confidence, and admiring a large engraving in 'The Cottager,' of 'A Dinner Party at the Zoo.' With tact, readiness, and good nature, some necessary Christian lessons are conveyed; for the city missionary, who has a genius as well as a heart for his work, is the most surprising object a novice is likely to meet with during an evening tour through London streets. Those waiters, for instance, can laugh and chat—laughing and chatting seem to make up their native language —but they can look serious too when some good thing is sent direct to their hearts. Leaving these, and turning the corner, we enter a capacious bar, a place which strikes one as being an interesting portion of the territory we are so strangely invading. The area being large and the company numerous, the servants can allow us but small attention, though each takes a paper, and returns a kindly recognition. The landlord here so unmistakably favours the work of Christian visitation, that a collecting box for the funds of the City Mission is constantly kept in use. There is a Babel-like confusion of conversation, combined with a clatter and clinking of pots and glasses, which at first is likely to make one involuntarily ask if this be not a strange place wherein to speak of Christ and to read His words. What do the people themselves think about the question? Mr. Landlord, who is far too considerable a person to be visible other than in his representatives, says, by his general approval, 'Do these people whatever good you can.' As regards the servants, they really do value the attentions paid them, and would, if examined, acknowledge their obligations. But what say the people, the wider constituency of public-house customers? Opinions differ among these witnesses on this, as on all other questions of the age. Listen a moment to those two young fellows who are pushing their way towards the bar: they are quietly expressing to one another their disapproval of obtruding religion into a public-house. *Per contra,* turn your attention to that gentleman in an opposite corner, and who is too far removed from the last speakers to catch their observations. He looks like a

7 *

man who prides himself in knowing what's
what, and now he advances the outspoken
opinion that 'Religion ain't no disgrace to
nobody.' The tracts, of which there is an
abundant supply, are now in requisition. Here
is one called 'Peaceful and Happy.' 'Ay,
"Peaceful and Happy," that's your style,
governor;' and the man who, maybe, thinks
that it ought to be his style, accepts the little
messenger, confessing that the *brochure* does
not describe his condition. Then there is the
history of 'Polly Pond, the Miner's Wife;' and
the 'ladies' tract' is well received by those for
whom it was prepared. '"Sounding Brass;"
"Sounding Brass." Who will have that?'
One here, and another there, until that finds
favour also. '"Poor Tom;" where is he to be
found? "Poor Tom"—any one here named
Tom?' 'My name's Tom.' 'Ah, there you
are.' The namesake of 'Poor Tom' is a tall,
wiry-looking man, not far advanced past middle

age. He takes the tract with a show of civil satisfaction, and as his name corresponds with the title, he finds much to say, and with considerable volubility proves to the company that he can form an opinion for himself. He had even heard a sermon from the Hon. and Rev. Baptist Noel, and having once been coachman to a well-known shipowner at Tottenham, who fitted up one of the first missionary ships, he appeared to think he had more than ordinary claim on our Christian regard, and complained of my companion's want of consideration in not having called upon him at his own house, and hoped to enjoy the pleasure of seeing him before long. It may be remarked here, once for all, that in this and other instances, the private addresses of several persons were taken down, to be visited at their homes during the ensuing week.

There is no one in this bar who ventures to decry the word which is boldly, and, it may be said, nobly spoken. Would any one fully realise the weight and authority of God's truth, they would do well to embrace an opportunity of hearing it proclaimed to a rough congregation, like that of a tavern bar on a Saturday night. There is no time for trifling or for showing off; for, distrusting the best words he can command, the evangelist will again and again fall back on the very words of Scripture. To say that I myself, as an admiring onlooker, was instructed and edified, is not to say much; and hence the encouraging comments, too lowly spoken to reach my companion's ear, came as a welcome testimony. 'I hold with a man like that,' said a young man of the mechanic class, to another of his own station. 'And so do I: there's no kid about it,' was the ready answer. These bar frequenters are illiterate and devoid of taste, but they can prize honesty and courageous endeavours to do them good. Oppose their prejudices by direct appeals to the Bible, and you may often gain an easy conquest over them.

'A good beginning,' I said, when we again breathed the pure air of the street.

Well, yes, my companion thought so too. He signified that the work must be taken as it comes. At times some profitable conversation is secured; at other times he is doomed to disappointment.

Pursuing our way, we next confront a large establishment which, as an omnibus station, and in other respects being a house occupying a commanding position, is said to be worth twenty thousand pounds in the open market. Though a regular attendant at public worship, and one who encourages his *employés* to copy a good example at least once on the Sabbath, Mr. Landlord does not wholly close on the day of rest, the receipts being too large to allow of his making the sacrifice. Though not numerous, the company here retains some special traits of interest. There stands a man at one end of the bar, with a half-finished glass of ale before him, who strikes one as being ' a character.' He is of middle age, and his countenance still bears those traces of refine-ment which arise from education. Instinct-ively, it would seem, he stands alone, and so keeps aloof from the vulgar herd of the street. Our entrance seemed to awaken him into good humour, for he at once became quite affable, his conversation being free from any profane or even coarse expressions. ' Give me the cast of your eye!' he cried, in rapid, authoritative tones. My companion at once looked the man straight in the face, and received his thanks for being so readily obliging. This stranger, who seemed to have made the human eye a special study, said that while the features in general might alter, the expression of the organs of vision remained virtually the same throughout life. He grew really excited on this harmless topic, and laid down many rules for the preservation of sight, which were not without interest and value to students. Yet, after he had observed how divers periodicals were handed over the counter, the tracts appeared to occasion him some perplexity. Who were we, and in what did our business consist? We might belong to a respectable species of colporteurs, or we might be of a genus of which he had never heard in the great world of money-getting. When he was offered a tract he rather awkwardly hesitated, and then, in a polite undertone, declined taking one, because—well, yes, if the truth must be told, his features seemed to say—because 'I have no money to-night.' When assured that the distribution was entirely gratuitous, he gladly took a copy, though even then he manifested signs of impatience at remarks upon religion, or concerning what in his vocabulary was equivalent—theology. Another person in this house, second only in interest to the genteel-looking stranger, was the barman, whose face brightened when the missionary went up to the counter. The poor fellow was in trouble, being about to resign his situation in consequence of being physically unequal to the heavy toil and the excessively protracted hours attached to Sabbathless weeks. The hours of service required of the *employés* in some of the more frequented taverns are amply sufficient for a double set of hands; and were landlords more humanely sensitive in this direction, a double set would be provided where one set is now overtaxed. The position of these people is frequently not far removed from slavery. They have no time for self-improvement; there are no opportunities of attending public worship, for were they to attend, as sometimes desired, they would find it impossible to keep awake through the sermon. To the mind of a man like our friend the barman, the ordinary working hours of bricklayers and carpenters are as easy as could be desired. With the weekly half-holiday, those hours preclude all necessity for opening museums and picture galleries on the Sabbath, consequent on want of time to attend them during the week. That barman, a smart, good-looking, active young fellow, said he would be glad enough to get a situation at twenty-three shillings a week, and escape the thraldom of the bar.

Still pursuing our way, we are everywhere civilly received, the *employés* in the bars of the larger houses still giving us a genial welcome, but to refer to every character met with would be impossible in a limited space. Here is seen, in one group, a respectable-looking widow, a modest-looking girl, and a young fellow who is treating them to stout. Though the widow, as a portly person, can evidently take her couple of glasses without inconvenience, the girl holds the glass daintily in her gloved hand, laughs at every witty remark of her protector, the gallant swain, and affects coyness in general. These accept our tracts, and listen respectfully to what is said. Then we encounter a woman, who, coming in for a jug of beer, says she is glad to see the missionary abroad; while in the same place is a cabman much depressed in mind, consequent on his child having been lately drowned in a water-tank, and his heart being soft, he listens to kind Christian advice with apparent thankfulness. The tracts are still eagerly received by old and young, only one man during our evening round openly refusing to accept the Gospel message. Many of the people even manifest a kind of pride in showing tracts received on former occasions, and take some trouble to explain that the papers are never destroyed. The children, also, are always remembered, and in one house a little girl comes forward to seek her portion of religious literature.

In front of one bar, among the crowd, stands
a young man, who, being civil, and even com-
plimentary, assures us he detected our business
as soon as we entered. His mind is stored
with texts of Scripture, learned at a Sabbath-
school, and his views of the plan of salvation
are also in the main correct—too correct, indeed,
to suit the taste of an argumentative individual
standing by, whose judgment is probably more
trustworthy as regards beer than as regards
theology. Two or three yards away, several
workmen, with pipes and pots, surround a
large barrel, and one of these, observing what
attention others are receiving, grows jealous,
suspecting he will be overlooked, and so he
steps forward to attract notice. These men
speak their mind in a rough and ready
manner, and with a pleasant freedom from
improper language. Speak of man's duty in
reading the Bible; one of these declares that
he does not know that he ever read a chapter

of Scripture during his life. Speak of man's corrupt heart; another says that he knows his heart is evil, because it has again and again led him astray. He may give up drinking for a time, to put himself financially straight, but then his evil heart, as he confesses, leads to his again breaking in upon the store. Uneducated, outspoken men, who will confess so much as this, may be nearer to the kingdom of heaven than their respectable neighbours suspect.

Such was our experience in the larger taverns. We now turned attention to houses of a much inferior class, and situated in the back streets, each being a rendezvous of dustmen and others, who, as a thirsty clan, are considerable customers. The landlord of one of these places is mentioned as ranking among the few who opposed the operations of the missionary on the occasion of his first calling. The house itself immediately strikes one as being a decidedly unpleasant place. Mr. Landlord being an intemperate, depraved character, the customers are also of a low order; and one might be excused for feeling ill-at-ease in the evil precincts of such a bar. On looking round the frowsy interior, nothing is discovered which tends to make vice more sightable. Everything repels one by its frowning gloom; the company, even, consisting of a man and a woman, separated by the length of the bar, being the most uncanny people met with during the evening. Mark well that man, if he really be a man. To the unassisted eye he resembles a reeking bundle of rags, whence issue forth sounds of imbecile merriment, the laughter evidently being provoked by my companion's kindly inquiries after Mr. Landlord's health. Poor old creature! We must regard him with pity rather than with contempt, even though he wear the drunkard's uniform, and does not, to judge by external evidence, patronize soap and water, at the most prosperous of seasons. He laughed internally, making little noise, and another fit of merriment occurred on his taking a tract, and listening to some remarks addressed directly to himself. He seemed to think religion, and all connected with religion, the funniest things on earth, Anon, he refers to his 'missus' and 'gal,' making one shudder involuntarily to hear of such a creature's possessing either wife or daughter. Yet while the Son of man comes to seek such as are lost, who shall say that the Gospel is spoken to such outcasts in vain?

In other-beerhouses the usual fraternity of dustmen were found congregating in force. Though in many instances they were noisy and profane, the fact must be placed to their credit that they offered no direct incivility or opposition to our progress; they were even pressingly hospitable, and seemed unable to understand the fortitude and self-denial on our part which successfully resisted their importunity to partake of a rich Saturday night concoction of ale and ginger-beer. This dustmen's district, as it may be called, was formerly very effectively served by one who some years since went to his rest, and it was striking as well as affecting to find how the good missionary's memory is cherished and honoured by the rough people who were once his constituents. In one beerhouse, and then in another, men and women paid voluntary tributes of respect to the memory of Henry Pearson.

The men patronising their favourite houses, are often found with their wives, muddling their brains and squandering their resources by drinking inordinate quantities of spirits and beer.

The reader will perhaps now admit that the beershop on a Saturday night is not only a legitimate sphere of missionary action, but

is a place likely to supply some phases of
street-life alike useful and interesting to legis-
lators and philanthropists. The house we are
now entering is crowded, the hour-hand of the
clock is fast approaching eleven, and some
of the company have taken rather more than
is good for them, though no cases of far-gone
drunkenness are observable. The women are
numerous, and are of the slatternly genus, but,
unthrifty as they are, they can speak a good
word for the well-remembered Henry Pearson.
'Polly Pond,' as 'a lady's book,' finds favour
among them, as do other similar productions.
An old fellow comfortably reclining on a bench
shows a disposition to be boastful of his good
sight and reading powers, but is soon compelled
to apologise for his inability to spell out
a couple of lines from 'Poor Tom.' Yes,
it is true that he is growing old, and his eyes
are becoming treacherous, and so, holding the
tract at arm's length, he remarks, 'Well,

sir, yer see, I've 'ad a little beer to-night.'
How much drink under such circumstances
might be accounted 'a little,' it was not
possible to learn, though his wife admitted,
'He've 'ad a good deal, sir.' They were
not willing to admit that they ever committed
any flagrant sin. 'Though we hev a little
beer, we don't do no 'arm; we don't thieve,
nor rob nobody,' remarked the woman who
spoke before. 'Ah, but drunkards shall not
inherit the kingdom of God,' replies my
companion.

As we elbow our way about the crowd in the
hot, smoky atmosphere, the tracts continue
to be civilly received, and remarks, humorous
and otherwise, are offered for our enlighten-
ment and entertainment. A dark-complex-
ioned gentleman, whose height does not greatly
exceed five feet, evinces considerable irritation
at being publicly pointed out as 'an old snob.'
Then followed honourable explanations. In

8 *

his youthful days that man was taken by the hand and started in life by the good missionary Henry Pearson, and Henry Pearson placed him at the shoemaking craft, besides giving him much valuable instruction and advice. It may not be desirable to have one's private history proclaimed from the housetops, or, what may be equivalent, to have one's secrets published in a thronged beerhouse on a Saturday night, but with a look combining scorn and injured innocence, the late 'snob' insists that 'a man *must* rise.' Had his knowledge been greater, he might have named several worthy men who have risen, and risen none the less honourably because they also once were called 'snobs.' Go where you may, you find members of two of our most useful crafts, those of the tailor and the shoemaker, subjected to odium on account of their calling. What is the reason for this?

We did not conclude our evening round

without gaining at least one welcome piece of information. Itinerants who visit among the lower orders in the manner described have abundant reason for encouragement, and have grounds for the hope of God's one day reviving His work in the world. How must civilisation have progressed even among the masses since the times of early Methodism, when ribald mobs sought every opportunity of opposing and maltreating those who desired their present and eternal good. The very words of Scripture are now spoken or read in public-houses by men whom even the most depraved respect for their work's sake. To accompany one of these evangelists for the purpose of watching his work is sure to excite your admiration, and may also prove bracing to your finer instincts, by strikingly revealing the hidden power lying within the words of Inspiration. In our late visit we were more than well received, and more than civilly treated. The worth of holy things was openly recognised. One brawny fellow, who begged for a copy of 'Mother's Last Words,' stoutly maintained that that highly popular tract was the best thing in our language, and a production which no man, however steeled his heart, could listen to without tears; a rash affirmation, perhaps, as coming from one whose acquaintance with literature was not of the broadest kind. Who, however, could do otherwise than respect such a man's opinion? I was glad to hear that preference for a good little book boldly spoken in a London beershop, at 10·45 p.m., on a Saturday night.

It is not too much to say that the most demoralising scene we visited during the entire evening was a music-hall in a main thorough-fare. There we saw an agency in active working order, warranted to ruin young persons surely and swiftly. The confusion and noise in the gilded and expensively-decorated bar were indescribable, while in the great hall, the admission to which was one shilling, there were, perhaps, over a thousand persons present. There were brilliant lights, sensual scenery, skilfully-performed music, and questionable songs, besides intoxicants *ad libitum*, such as each chose to order. What more potent means could be devised for encompassing the moral overthrow of the young, especially of inexperienced and unsuspecting girls, who are too often blindly led into the fatal arena?· One need not hesitate in denouncing tavern music-halls as breeders of moral pestilence, and as an abuse of the liberty awarded by the State to licensed victuallers. Undoubtedly such places should be summarily dealt with by the legislature. In no well-ordered community should low concert-rooms and drinking-saloons be allowed to combine and work together in their work of corrupting the people; and were the licensing powers of each parish handed over to the vestry, those whose families are imperilled by the present state of things might have a chance of checking a growing evil. Very few publicans, comparatively, have music licenses, so that, happily, these remarks affect but a small section of the trade. Concerning the Christian visitation in general of their houses, I repeat that the mission is a noble attempt to reach the masses, many of whom, perhaps, would not be easily reached by any other road. The public needs only to become more fully acquainted with the working of the public-house mission, to award it their support, their sympathy, and, above all, their prayers.

If the commencement of the public-house mission was not so auspicious as the too sanguine anticipated, its earliest fruits gave promise of a more plentiful harvest in the future. It is to my mind both remarkable and encouraging that the first coster, whom the pioneer tavern missionary accosted in a

London bar, should have become a Christian; and should afterwards have died, exclaiming, 'Christ died for poor me, and He has made it all right now, and I shall go up to Him.' I think there is something equally consoling in the fact that the landlord of the first house entered by the first-appointed missionary to the publicans, should have surrendered to the Gospel. The man showed a disposition to be violent and abusive, and the best welcome he afforded the missionary was to seize him by the arm, and, with curses, push him out of doors. On falling ill, this man became glad of the Christian attentions so lately abused, proved himself a really changed character, and died at length a triumphant death.

My friend himself gained the acquaintance-ship of a landlord who doggedly set himself against Christianity, and refused to see any Christian counsellor, until persuaded to do so by a brother publican, to whom the missionary had been made useful. The sick man listened to the Gospel message, repented, and believed. Change of air being necessary in his still weak state of health, friends advised his removing to a shooting-box which he owned a few miles out of London. 'No,' he replied, 'I cannot do that, for if once I get down there, my old companions will surround me, and the temptation will be too strong.' The sincerity of his conversion was seen when he sold the estate, together with its dogs, horses, and guns. This man likewise subsequently died rejoicing in a good hope through Christ.

Having now given in detail some impressions taken during a Saturday evening round in company with an energetic public-house missionary, some other particulars of the every-day work of the same agent may very properly follow. I give my friend credit for being a ready wit and smart at repartee. He is well aware that no evangelist can have better opportunities of utilising general knowledge than one in his position, and he shapes his action accordingly. Supposing, *e.g.*, that, as in the present instance, the battle-field is Paddington, he will take care to store his mind with such local history as can be readily found, as well as with other miscellaneous information. He knows when certain streets and squares were erected, what persons of note in bygone times resided in the vicinity, and he can speak about the fashionable taverns and pleasure-gardens as they existed in the time of Queen Anne. He recollects what duels were fought when the area was in a great part open fields, and he can recite many very interesting inscriptions on tombstones in the parish church. It may not always be expedient to press religion on a stranger's notice at the first moment of meeting, and hence the gift is profitably cultivated which enables a man to become an entertaining companion on the shortest notice.

It is well known that many of the more considerable publicans are holders of very valuable property in a commercial sense. Immense sums are expended in the erection of large taverns, and still greater capital would be necessary to purchase the lease and good-will of some of their commanding sites. Concerning the landlords of these establishments, we may safely confide in the testimony of men who as evangelists spend their time among them and their customers; and these men assure us that, taken as a whole, the upper class of publicans are a good, moral-living, and hospitable race, who attend well to their families, and generously support the licensed victuallers' institutions. Still, the truth must be confessed that some few others of the publican world are scarcely alive to any sense of propriety, and care little whose ruin they encompass if only their selfish ends are gained. Of the want of moral principle among such we are able to judge from a notice like the following, exhibited to tempt those to indulge in greater excess whose besetting sin is drinking:—

'For this day only. Notice! On Sunday, April 8th. Meux's splendid porter, $2\frac{1}{2}$d. per pot; Finest Old Tom, $3\frac{1}{2}$d. per quartern; Jamaica rum, 4d. per quartern. Not less than a pot of beer or a quartern of spirits at the above prices. No change will be given.'

Characters who can descend to these low tactics require managing with considerable tact. Then my friend is no stranger to odd, or even to tragic occurrences, which happen on his wide district. Fancy, for example, that you see a company of enterprising roughs who have planned a novel kind of 'lark.' They watch Mr. Landlord leave his house— the one they themselves frequent — then immediately enter, overpower the landlady, and regale themselves to the full with spirits and cigars. Fancy, further, that when these gentlemen are prosecuted, their indignant 'pals' cease using the prosecutor's house, and so oblige his retiring to another part of the town. All this has been known to occur. An unfortunate barmaid has even had a preparation of pepper thrown in her eyes, for the sake of facilitating another robbery.

But we may look a little further into my friend's work, which, being extremely diversified, meets with ever-varying success. To-day, a beam of sunshine darts down suddenly and unexpectedly; to-morrow, comes rebuff and discouragement. The reader must now suppose the time to be a little after nine on a Sabbath evening; the place being a narrow, uninviting street at the west end of the town. In the sombre shade of this thoroughfare stands one of those public-houses of questionable repute, where people assemble who have more than a taint of suspicion resting on their character. The landlord of a den like this must be judiciously and kindly dealt with. You cannot respect him, but to excite his ire by telling him so would be to defeat your own purpose. The missionary, however, who has common sense as well as tact, and knows how to ingratiate himself into the confidence of landlords and their subordinates of every shade of temper, walks forward into an inner room, where are congregated some thirty men and women of loose moral habits, and whose business is thieving. They are taken suddenly by surprise, occupied as they are in their Sabbath recreation of gaming, drinking, and, perhaps, concocting plans for future depredations. 'Hallo; who's this cove?' calls out one of the most sensitive of the gang, in sentinel-like tones. 'All right, gentlemen; don't disturb yourselves,' is the reply. 'I've brought you some capital little books.' There is ever something tempting in books, even to the most illiterate. Those who cannot read them like looking at the engravings, and asking what the pictures are about. The case of tracts is at once opened, several pairs of eyes curiously watching the process. 'Who'll have this?' calls out my intruding friend, holding up that readable poetical production, 'Oh, if I were the Squire?' 'That's my tract,' answers an idle-looking fellow, who at once accepts the paper. But that black case contains an ample supply of 'ladies' books' also, and care is taken to distribute these wisely and liberally. Now there comes uppermost another readable-looking article, 'Trust the Pilot.' 'Ah, ah!' cries a sailor, or a quondam sailor, among the throng, awakened into consciousness by a nautical allusion. 'Ah, ah!' Why the gen'l'm's got his eyes on a brother tar. Hand that here, and give us one for a mate.'

In such a company the tracts are almost invariably well received, and a text of Scripture is usually repeated in each instance.

The seed thus sown will sometimes show symptoms of yielding fruit even at the season of sowing. See, now, there is a man who is revolving in his mind some words from the New Testament he has just been hearing. 'Guv'nor!' he cries, 'you told me when you gave me this book that if I'd believe in Jesus Christ I should be saved. Now just tell me how we're to do that?" Rejoicing in any favourable signs, and especially glad to hear a straightforward question asked in such a godless company, the evangelist compliments the man for being honestly open, and is proceeding to reply more particularly, when the clatter and confusion of tongues well-nigh drowns his voice, and at least prevents his being heard.

'Silence, there!' roars one of the most interested of the audience; while another, prompted to interfere by love of order, threatens to break the heads of any who do not cease talking. ' Silence, there! question's asked, and gen'l'm's goin' to give a answer.'

One who can provoke a crisis like this needs to be in command of both knowledge and wisdom. Without desiring to pay compliments, I may say that I have never observed a city missionary fail in showing a readiness of utterance at the proper time. In the present instance a concise explanation of the Gospel followed, made plainer by being accompanied with what all easily comprehend—an illustration from daily life. All in that room had heard about the fever which had broken out in the workhouse yonder. Now, suppose there were two men in one ward, and both alike, ill—both alike lying at death's door. The doctor knows of one medicine which will cure them, and of only one, and that is infallible. Strange to say, while the restoring draught is freely offered to both patients, one, while knowing of its healing power, refuses to drink, and consequently dies. The other is more eager to recover. He knows this to be his only chance of life; he dreads death; he drinks and lives. Well, now, everybody is infected by a worse poison than typhus, for all have sinned. Yes, all have sinned, and unless we go to the Physician of souls we shall surely die of our disease. Jesus Christ is the Physician who offers the water of life, and unless we go to Him, unless we drink and live, we shall surely perish. It is not possible to give all which was spoken on either side, nor were all alike willing listeners. Interruptions came from the players, and were peremptorily opposed by ' Shut up!' from one who was interested; while another would call out, ' Go on, guv'nor; he's a fool, and can't understand; you never mind 'im.' Difficult work is that of speaking to a congregation of outcasts; but realising the importance of sending something home to their hearts, the good evangelist counts himself happy when able to rise to the occasion.

But some progress is surely being made; a spirit of inquiry is awakened, for numbers gather round to see and hear what is going on.

'Look here!' cries an ill-dressed man, who is at least possessed of curiosity, if not of a longing after good. · 'Look here, I wasn't always the cove I am; I once had a good suit of toggery. Well, in them days I was 'vited to go and 'ear a parson called F——, somewhere up Maida-hill way. He preached on two women; one he said was Martha, and t'other he called Mary. He told us just what sort of women they were. One of the women stuck to her work like a brick; but the other dropped her broom, and began to jaw just like a woman. Now, what I want you to tell us, guv'nor, is this: The parson said in one place, " One thing is needful," and he never told us what it was, and I could never make it out. It's been up and down in my mind many a time. You explain that to us, like you did that other question, and let's 'ave a illustration.'

How good illustrations do tell by striking home to the heart! The people now listen to an account of a ship in a storm. She strikes on a rock; she springs a leak; she threatens to sink, and drown her crew. What is the 'one thing needful' for a sinking ship? 'A life-boat!' Yes, that's right; a life-boat. 'I'm a wreck,' continues the speaker; 'that woman's a wreck; the great waves of sin are fast drowning us. "One thing is needful." There is a life-boat for us, a refuge for us, a Saviour for us. He is able to save unto the uttermost. A drowning man once cried out, "Lord, save me!" and immediately Jesus stretched forth His hand and caught him. It was the "one thing needful."'

Characters whom we too readily regard as so far sunk in moral degradation as to be irrecoverable, are not beyond the reach of God. They are not indisposed to listen to the Gospel if the truth be presented in a becoming way. It might defeat his purpose were their instructor to approach and cry out indignantly, ' You are going to hell!' But if he will point out to them the road to heaven, he will get willing listeners even in a thieves' rendezvous. ' Goodnight, guv'nor,' cry out the men: ' come again soon, and give us another stunning lecture.'

My friend now goes further afield, and probably does not proceed far without meeting with one of the most obstinate members of the human genus, who is prejudiced against religion because of the inconsistencies of Christian professors. The gentleman's servant, as we meet with him in tavern parlours, is a study worthy of the pencil of Hogarth. He is pompous, affected, and prouder than his master, and were his acquaintance with English more perfect, he would not be more entertaining. One of these will look with disfavour on Christianity because the bishop of so-and-so, the duke of this or that, and my lady something else, are oné and all inconsistent. *They* ride in their carriages to church; *they* indulge in every kind of luxury; they do many other things which James cannot emulate. Anon, another objector to the tracts appears. He is a Romanist, and dislikes Protestant tracts because there is nothing in them about 'the Mother of God.' These all call for kindly persuasion, argument, and warning. Though the good results springing from the constant effort put forth are smaller than we could wish, they are still large enough to bring encouragement and reward.

Probably the missionary is not more unpopular with any class than with those fast young men who, though frequenters of taverns, affect gentlemanly airs, and make brave endeavours to atone for want of understanding, and general emptiness of mind, by foppish display, and claiming to come of a gentle origin. Let us notice a couple of this description who appear on the scene during a Sabbath evening in summer. The neighbourhood is wealthy, being bounded by one of the West-end parks, and streams of well-dressed people are going and coming in all directions, and enjoying the air. The two fast youths enter a large tavern where my friend happens to be standing. Look well at them, and your eyes must be untrained, indeed, in observing different phases of street life, if you do not instantly see through the disguise which the cheap tailor and the haberdasher have been able to provide, and beneath the thin veil you detect low-bred vulgarity peeping out to mock at pretty actions and pretentious words. While some specimens of this species may work for their bread, others, perhaps, procure what cash is necessary for meeting daily engagements in ways they prefer not to have explained; but, in either instance, they are small fry whose recreation consists in persecuting unwilling barmaids with 'attentions' and small talk. The poor girls could do well without this patronage, and would, perhaps, be more determined in resisting, were they not compelled to keep an eye on an employer's profit. If you inspect the hats and canes of these gentry—and they expect all to look at them—you may reasonably ask yourself if the manufacturers of such superb articles should not rapidly rise in popular estimation. There is surely no doubt about the finish and the style. Even the very movements of these gay butterfly personages are calculated to attract observation. Their actions speak truer language than their tongues. What practice must be needed ere one can assume that graceful posture in public; and who else beside the man at your elbow could rap his nose just like that with the head of a dainty cane, or drink a glass of ale from first to last so precisely like a connoisseur? Well-dressed, handsome bar-maids act like potent forces in inspiring the little minds of these little men.

'A beautiful evening, miss,' remarks one of the fast little men, in blandest tones. 'We're just taking an airing round the park. Suppose you don't often get out? Great pity! Your company would have much enhanced our pleasure. Female society greatly adds to the beauties of nature. Any evening you're likely to be disengaged, and will honour us with your company, it will greatly add to our felicity.' The girl bows, my friend, meanwhile, harbour-ing doubts as to the wisdom of offering tracts to these full-blown gents. He begins to question whether he will not be annihilated in the blaze of so much display. However, he ventures to be sufficiently bold to offer a tract, 'The Lamp kept always Burning.' The fast little man shapes his features into an expression of high disdain; he smiles sarcastically, and then speaks in the best wit his little brains can muster. 'What a queer title — "The Lamp kept always Burning." I suppose that is intended for young married men who stay out late at night, and keep up their poor wives burning the candle?' Then he does worse than make small puns; he waxes profane, and provokes some well-deserved rebukes, until, weak as he is morally and intellectually, he perceives the policy of apologising, and even of promising to read the tract. Barmaids who are beset by customers of this sample, if they themselves possess any strength of character, value the talk of such worthless admirers as they value the meaningless chatter of parrots. They shrink in disgust from their familiarity, and regard them with general contempt.

My friend, however, cannot afford to regard even one of his constituents with aught ranking lower than pity. He knows that if some of these youthful pretenders could be followed in their life-course, a few more years would show the bloom and even the gaiety of life to have vanished. There is no longer any romance linked with life when a man's dissipation and general fastness of living have come to an abrupt termination by wearing out the frame. See yonder man with a broken arm, standing in front of a bar, where a number of 'pals' have 'treated' him into semi-senselessness. That man has let slip fair opportunities. The tide of life, which taken at the flood would have led on to fortune, has subsided never to rise again; and what is still worse, his parents are found descending with their grey hairs in sorrow to the grave. 'This is a friend of ours,' remarks one of the men, alluding to the broken-armed simpleton. 'He's been in a good bit of pain, so we thought it would be a charity to give him something to drink, and so you see we've made him drunk. Can you do anything for him? His case is a real one, take our word for it. We wouldn't tell a lie.' 'The money you've spent during the last hour would have helped him far more than anything I can do,' answers my friend. 'Well, so it would, that's true, only we didn't think of it till you gave us these tracts,' adds the man.

Now look into a poor home, where are a broken-hearted mother and a stricken father, the man lying ill in bed. 'Oh, sir, it must be my son you mean,' cries the old man, as my friend seats himself by the bed, and refers to the broken-armed simpleton. 'He's not been home since Sunday. He often stays out all night, and there is no telling what company he is with. I was a linen-draper once, and comfortably off, but our son cost us in one year between seventy and eighty pounds. He went into the army, and the navy, and has given us no end of trouble and sorrow. He has met with a dreadful accident now, but it hasn't made him better. Soon he is going to be married to a very respectable and good young woman, who has saved some money, and supports her old mother in the country. We all hope he'll be better then, and start in business and get on.' The poor old people became much affected when kindly spoken to, and are addressed in the words of the twenty-third Psalm. That 'a very respectable and good young woman' should be closely associated with such a scene, is one of those anomalies of life too often met with in London.

It will not be supposed that the aim of the public-house missionary is merely to benefit the customers of publicans. He looks well after these, and is rewarded by attracting the attention of casual passengers, but his mission is also a special one to the publicans themselves and to their servants. Among these he has an extensive auditory, and, through advising them, he is their valued counsellor and friend. He can tell of publicans who have become Christian converts through his instrumentality, and of barmaids and barmen who have admitted that only by reading what has been put into their hands, and by acting upon the advice offered, have they been saved from the ruin to which they are continually exposed. Then there is another class to whom the precepts of the Bible come like life-salvation, the widows of deceased publicans, who, occupying covetable business positions, attract an inconvenient number of undesirable admirers. These women are peculiarly subject to annoyance from shameless and worthless adventurers, who come with proposals of marriage, and to be of service to such unprotected females is to reap at least some reward. 'I hope God will keep me from making a fool of myself,' exclaimed one woman who was thus tormented. Hence, admitting his honesty of purpose in visiting them, the publicans commonly encourage their friend's visits, there being but one house out of four hundred wherein objections to his calling are raised. The licensed victuallers are far from ignoring religion. Their chief school is conducted on Christian principles, having a duly qualified chaplain, and an annual sermon, while every child who leaves the institution is presented with a copy of the Bible.

To give in detail every instance of individual good received — the fruits of this mission — which has come within my knowledge, would too greatly extend the limits of this article. Hopeless as it may seem to go into taprooms to distribute tracts among the profane, the sensual, and the illiterate; or to invade ' parlours,' to drop the good seed of the Kingdom among the fast living and the opinionated, experience proves that the work is not hopeless. In front of yonder bar stands a young man half intoxicated, but still able to take home a well-deserved rebuke for using profane words. Is *he* quite a lost character? If any are too far gone to be recoverable, surely you may conclude they are such as he. Now he becomes sufficiently communicative to give his name and address. He is a well-to-do middle-class man, living in his own house, and respectably connected. On being visited, he is found to be in an exceedingly dejected state of mind, and he makes an open confession: 'I am a ruined and lost man! My wife has been crying ever since Sunday night! I can never trust myself again! I cannot tell what possessed me! I always go to church, and my children to a Sunday-school. When I went out the night you met with me, I had no intention of taking anything to drink, but meant to attend a place of worship. No one persuaded me to go to a public-house, and I cannot tell what led to so much wickedness. After you left I got into the worst of company, and was so drunk that I couldn't walk home. My poor wife was frightened when she saw me, and she says I called her the most shocking names, and threatened to ill-use her. If I go out alone I may very likely do the same thing again.'

What good signs are fear and grief in a transgressor. That man was counselled with the wisdom of the good Old Book, and though the peace which he needed, and which his friend longed to welcome, was long in coming, it did come at last, and the man, lately overtaken in a fault, became a changed character. He grew even anxious for the conversion of friends, and not long since he undertook a long journey for the sake of offering Christian consolation or instruction to an ailing relative.

Many striking and pleasing circumstances come directly beneath the notice of my active friend, the tavern evangelist. Numbers of private histories with which he necessarily becomes acquainted are of a character such as render it neither prudent nor kind to give them publicity, while of others a bare outline has to suffice, so as not to give unnecessary offence. He points out a certain house where there lived a widow, who, to personal charms, added the substantial attractions of a thriving trade, and four thousand pounds in ready money. This woman was wooed, and actually won, by a rascally French adventurer, who at once left his wife to mourn over her folly in having heeded his beguiling words. As a welcome set-off against this, is the case of a man who, having forsaken the religion of his fathers during thirty years, was reclaimed to God and virtue by means of a word spoken in a tavern, one Sabbath evening, whither he had gone to procure some refreshment. Here is found a quondam publican, who relinquished his trade after reading

a book lent him by the indefatigable agent.*
Still more pleasing, in another place, is
a Christian worker—a publican's daughter—
who, having a tract district of her own,
is a regular visitor among the poor.

Seeing so much as he does of life, and well
understanding the power of the Gospel, as
well as the obstacles which truth has to
overcome, my friend, I am delighted to find,
is neither an optimist nor a pessimist. He
is a hard worker, who is fully alive to the
magnitude and importance of the warfare
engaged in by the City Mission; and yet
he is not accustomed to take too sombre views
of the situation in London. Seeing what
he does, he thinks truth is prevailing, and
is destined to prevail. If we ask what are
the chief discouragements in a work like this,

* Note by Mr. Spurgeon.—And a very sensible
man too, for this article shows what sort of a trade it
is. The most friendly eye cannot but mark the awful
perils which surround it.

we find out that there are things quite as seriously obstructive as the corrupt human heart. There are the writings of a deistical bishop, whose sense of honour does not prevent his living to spread abroad among the people a set of imbecile opinions. There are the vagaries and fooleries of Ritualism, and the grovelling notions of Divine truth held by the extreme broad-churchmen. Many of the poor are themselves as fully alive to the evils besetting them as are their instructors. Some of them, after embracing the Gospel, will, even in cases of sorest need, avoid applying to a minister at all, through fear of being attended by an aspiring Ritualist or a Jesuitical Romanizer. My friend tells of one good woman, who herself actually dispensed to a dying daughter the bread and wine, commemorative of Christ's dying love. She did this rather than risk having the unwelcome services of an assuming ecclesiastic whose religion had no worthier foundation than priestcraft and millinery. If she sinned by acting disorderly, who, in such times as ours, will venture on casting a stone at her?*

After what has been said, it is hoped that none of my readers will question the need existing for an agency like the public-house mission, on which the Divine blessing is manifestly resting. We may one and all congratulate the Church on being able to command the services of skilful and earnest men, who seek for spoil in places likely and unlikely. Seeing what I have seen of their daily toil and procedure, I believe in the honest sincerity of these men. Indeed, I have never doubted their devotedness to a high service, finding it difficult to suppose that Englishmen with able hands and common sense would choose

---

* NOTE BY MR. SPURGEON. — We see no disorder in it if she and her daughter were believers. It is flat Popery to suppose that a minister's presence is necessary at the communion.

the thankless profession of a city missionary merely for the sake of gaining a poor livelihood. What does England, as a nation, owe to modern town missions? Far more than the busy merchant or excited place - hunter allows himself time to calculate. To what depths of ruin would 'the dangerous classes' have sunk by this time had no missionary reclaimers set up their meetings among them, and had not such gained the confidence of the people by visiting them, and by attending the bedsides of their dying friends and relatives in close courts and alleys! And, to keep to the immediate subject in hand, what would the taverns of London become if cut off from every Christian influence, and if religion is to be set aside as so 'out of place in a public-house,' as some still loudly insist?

What public-houses might be, or what they really should be in a Christian country, is not the argument, and no word-picture of the kind need be attempted. Many taverns are far more respectably conducted than some persons are aware of, and Christian landlords are sometimes found behind the scenes. What, however, the gin-palace or low beerhouse is capable of becoming in less scrupulous hands, we also know. Is not the gin-palace a centre of evil, a place where the unholy passions of our fallen nature riot without check or hindrance? Is it not there that the depraved vent their blasphemy, and as slaves of lust or crime inflame their grovelling propensities by the readiest means at command? Is it not there that the simple and the unsuspecting are beguiled to take their fatal first step towards destruction, and do not the young there find the fence already broken down—the safeguards of virtue which fond parents had set about them before sending them forth into the uncertain world? Under the exciting influence of the reigning tyrant, Alcohol, is not female innocence betrayed or surrendered, and a thousand other things committed which degrade men to the level of devils? Who, then, would not have the warning voice raised even in the public-house, so that the hand of a Christian friend may at least bring some back into the good old way, or may be laid on the shoulder of some young, unsuspecting thing, to warn her from the precipice, on the edge of which she stands in unsuspicious gaiety? We can hail with acclamation a victory won even in a field like this; and while not classing landlords as a body with encouragers of vice, we know that some sink to that low level, and we also know that whether a landlord will have it so or not, bad characters of every name make a rendezvous of the public-house.

The Christian visitation of public-houses is a mission worthy of the Church. Nevertheless, how little is being done for want of labourers, and at a time when the people show a readiness unknown to former ages to listen to the Gospel. What are our rich and great provincial towns doing in this special work? What is Scotland—the land of hope in these days of Ritualistic declension—doing? We found no missionary to the Edinburgh whiskey shops. Never in the history of the Church were there louder calls to action — to work while it is called to-day. Opportunities are here, they are quickly passing, and the night cometh when no man can work.*

* NOTE BY MR. SPURGEON.—These two papers upon tavern-visitation have been painfully interesting to us. We would not for a moment discourage the workers in such an atmosphere, but how needful is it to keep our fellow-men from entering into it! Will it always be so? Is the nation given over to drunkenness? It behoves Christian men to see that they make no gains by the ruin of souls, and use their best endeavours to discourage excess in every class of society.

III.

JEWS AND SABBATH MARKETERS.

JEWS AND SABBATH MARKETERS.

BY frequent visits to a place of worship in the vicinity, I formerly became more familiar than was pleasant
with the Sabbath morning bustle and ribaldry
of Petticoat-lane.   The peculiar hubbub occasioned by ten thousand Gentile and Hebrew
tongues, chaffing and bargaining, could not
only be heard distinctly in the pews, but the
price of a coat, or the proposed abatement
on a hat, was too audibly spoken not to interfere with the preacher's comfort as he officiated
in the pulpit.

Lament it as we may, as a stain on modern civilisation, the 'Lane' is an institution of low London; and the most popular preacher cannot hope to attract by eloquence and wit so vast a throng as gather here week by week to banter, bustle, jostle, and swear, under the presidency of the Lord of Misrule. The Jews, it is true, take the profit, but the Gentiles monopolise the fun. Two races, of opposite sympathies, meet in close proximity, for the ostensible purpose of serving each other. Roughs and thieves are here in shoals, though great numbers also assemble who pass for respectable mechanics. They are wanting cheap clothes, second-hand tools, or flash jewellery; and so while dinner is preparing, and while Mrs. Housewife is tidying the too narrow lodging for the festivities commencing at one p.m. — or, otherwise, with some select female companions, is discussing the delin- quencies of men in general, and those of her

own husband in particular,—the man himself
is getting more satisfaction and excitement
here than is obtainable in his own home. The
public-houses are closed, but refreshments
can be had. There are whelks, pickled salmon,
fish fried in oil, sweetmeats, sherbet, and if
you have no appetite for these, there are
medicines to create one; while to entertain
the mental faculties there are shouts, screams,
and whistling, each and all intended to signify
something, if only you have the capacity to
catch what that something may be.

Probably few easy-going middle-class people
would wish to share the hilarity of the ' Lane '
on market-day, as the Sabbath morning may be
called. Yet those who for any special purpose
desire to see the place at all, must go when the
crowd is in force, or in the Sunday forenoon,
when ten or twelve thousand persons are com-
puted to be present, and when you have to
push in a determined manner through the

throng, meanwhile getting pressed and jostled
rather roughly for your pains. Here are the
lower strata of the social fabric—' the dangerous
classes'—a sixth part of the whole being classed
with those who make thieving a profession, and
Sunday morning in this notorious market is
confessedly a harvest for the fraternity of pick-
pockets and cadgers. The majority, however,
are mechanics and labourers, who claim to be
accounted honest and respectable, but who
prefer passing the morning here in déshabille
to any other attraction, sacred or secular.
Thus buyers, sellers, idlers, and thieves make
up a motley company, which a lower civilisation
than ours, in a city like London, might reasonably have forbidden to assemble.

There are a number of policemen on the
ground, who would keep order were such an
achievement a thing among possibilities. Keep
order? In the 'Lane' law and decency may
be outraged with comparative impunity, the arm

of authority not being strong enough to inter-
pose check or hindrance. You need not necessarily possess a very keen eye to detect the
manner in which pocket-handkerchiefs migrate
from their owners' possession to the dealers'
pegs; while the ribald blasphemy and revolt-
ing obscenity which at every turn assail the
unwilling ears, makes a chance visitor wish for
the power of becoming deaf at will. What do
the police think of the business? 'How do you
like your office here?' one man was asked.
'We are obliged to like it,' he replied: 'they
claim it as a charter.'

After the church bells have ceased tolling
worshippers into their appointed places, the
'Lane' traffic reaches its height. The mere act
of taking a noontide view of the scene seems to
beget sensations of bewilderment, so that to understand what is going on it is necessary to give
attention to individual characters. There may
meet your eye a young thief, who has lately

succeeded in taking a haul, and perhaps he is offering to dispose of a gold chain for a sum six times less than its original worth. Then there at your elbow, talking with a low-browed, villanous-looking broker, are some experts at passing base coin, and who find this a convenient market for replenishing their stock. Note how hawk-eyed Jewish dealers are looking out for sellers as eagerly as for buyers. The majesty of the law is represented by a score or so of constables, more or less; but what cares this chaffing, bantering host for the blue uniforms of city police, when, as they would tell you, law is a luxury only suitable for well-to-do people? Robberies can be committed with impunity even under the eyes of the officers. The strong arm of justice may grasp at the offender, but, as a policeman once remarked, he has only to 'stoop down and cut away,' and capture becomes impossible. Under such circumstances it is useless to think of taking a thief; and Mr. Policeman pointedly adds, 'There are so many of them, that they cover one another.'

The market is a very general one. The faint-like effluvium peculiar to a London crowd does not overpower the more pleasant but by no means appetising odour of edibles, either in their natural state, or as prepared by the art and devices of Hebrew cooks. Stalls and baskets are laden with the bounties of the season, and only those seem to forego luncheon who have no means to pay for some of the variety of refreshments provided. Then more important wares are recommended in stentorian tones. If not already aware of the fact, you learn that 'Now's your time for a good tile.' You will be invited to lay in ample stores of stockings, books, slates, pencils, pictures, furniture polish, newly-invented blacking, medicines, ointments, and a thousand-and-one other things supposed to be necessary to human comfort in our present high state of civilization. It is an uproarious fair; and the eagerness with which trade is carried on by vendors, who seem to possess lungs of horse-power, is apparently stimulated by the remembrance that the harvest is as transient as morning sunshine, seeing poor people dine at one o'clock.

Some of the bargains effected are sufficiently ludicrous to interest the public. An evangelist who visits hereabout once watched a man negotiating for a pair of red-topped morocco boots, which, as the perquisites of some Jeames or other, may have found their way into this ready receptacle. The poor fellow's feet, not used to such smartly-cut articles, resisted the effort to pull them on; but the seller stood encouragingly by. 'Oh, you'll git them on in time, never fear, and they're jist the boots that'll wear.' The buyer at last succeeds in his endeavour, but does so to make an unwelcome discovery—'They're too long!' 'What's that you say?' retorts the woman. 'Too long? Not a bit of it, not a bit of it! They're jist your fit! It's all the fashion now to have 'em a bit too long in the toe!' That argument certainly carries some point, and partially reconciles the purchaser to what he in ignorance supposed to be a defect. The man now stands looking half admiringly, when, alas, a more damaging fact comes to light—'They're odd ones!' 'What's that you say?' indignantly cries the stall-keeper. 'Don't tell me that: 'tain't likely I'd come here to sell odd boots or shoes. I should not sell so many as I do if I sold odd ones. All my customers come again. Now they're a nice fit, young man; what's the most you'll give?' After this energetic speech a satisfactory termination to the business might have been expected; but in reply the man only makes the unchivalrous offer of 'two bob.' This ends the entire business, for with the contemptuous reproof,

'Do you think I stole 'em?' the lady flings away the goods, and the mechanic walks away. All this takes place while the citizens are comfortably seated in their churches and chapels, worshipping the God of purity, love, and peace. The atmosphere is charged with physical as well as moral poison. Yes, Petticoat-lane is a centre of moral pestilence in the first city of the world.

We may inquire, How did such an eyesore as the 'Lane' originate? Rag Fair was formerly established in Rosemary-lane, a thoroughfare leading from Tower-hill to St. George's-in-the-East, abounding in fever courts, and in the last century associated with the famous mystery of Elizabeth Canning. Petticoat-lane has lately changed its name to Middlesex-street; but this alteration is totally disregarded by the fraternity who compose the Sabbath concourse. The 'Lane' is likely to retain its old name so long as it continues a nuisance to the metropolis.

With one side bounding Whitechapel and the other belonging to the City proper, Middlesex-street has successfully rivalled the more ancient market of Rosemary-lane. One advantage prized by the present frequenters is the covered exchange, the fee to which is one halfpenny. Having been erected by a Jew, this has aided in increasing the traffic which seems to increase with the growth of the City, though in past times perhaps the disorder was even greater than at present. Some old attendants at a once celebrated chapel in the neighbourhood, remember times when Rag Fair encroached on the very precincts of the sanctuary, the Jews having tacked their wares on to the side wall of the chapel.

In regard to the trade of Rag Fair, it is somewhat extensive, while the scale of prices of wearing apparel and other articles is not without interest to the uninitiated. Several years ago a gentleman desired to supply funds to a city missionary for the purpose of his fitting out any deserving couple who were about marrying and starting in life. The donor's wishes, on being carried out, entailed an outlay which no less surprised himself than it conduced to the delight of the happy pair immediately concerned—the man's outfit costing three shillings and threepence, and the lady's trousseau three shillings and one penny, according to the details of the invoice:— 'A full-fronted shirt, very elegant,' cost sixpence, and light-coloured trousers, becoming so festive an occasion, were obtained for a like sum. Despising white waistcoats, one of black cloth was selected, and at the reasonable charge of threepence, while minor articles, such as braces, shoes, gloves, cap, &c., were in each instance put down at one penny. More important, and a garment entailing perhaps undue anxiety in selection, was the bridegroom's coat; but all difficulty was finally overcome by the timely choice of 'a black beaver fly-fronted, double-breasted paletot coat, lined with silk — a very superior article,' at eighteenpence. The bride's requisites were supplied on terms equally advantageous. The wedding dress cost tenpence; petticoats fourpence each, a head-dress twopence, stays twopence, and a shift one penny. The most considerable figure in the list, and one which nearly corresponded to the bridegroom's coat, was 'a lady's green silk paletot, lined with crimson silk, trimmed with black velvet, quilted and wadded throughout.' This also cost tenpence. On completing his settlement with the dealer, the good missionary found he had disbursed a sum of six shillings and fourpence, and it may be doubted if six shillings and fourpence ever produced more pleasure in the hearts of two needy people. As it was, the outlay considerably exceeded what it would have done had not the benefactor's instructions to his friend been imperative that he was not to be parsimonious.

This, then, is a field white unto the harvest for our London city missionaries to take possession of; and the unobtrusive earnestness, not to say frequent self-denying heroism, which they show in their work, is nobly encouraging. In this repulsive district a missionary some years ago was struck down by fever, after labouring in fetid courts and alleys during seven years, and what seemed strange, the disease occurred after his removal to a healthier sphere. 'In the lowest and most depraved parts of the district he was best known,' said his wife. 'The bed of sickness and the obscurest hole of wretchedness were where he loved best to be.' The last hours of this devoted man were happy, and his Christian triumph complete. Is not the enthusiasm of such as extraordinary as it is pleasing, and is not the grace which enables them to sacrifice themselves, and even

to love their tainted districts, as wonderful as
it is common? One agent, who laboured at a
close, foul station, not far from the 'Lane,'
was once found to be succumbing to bad air
and the ceaseless strain on the nervous system,
so that his committee decided on removing
him to a healthier spot. Most persons might
suppose that one so situated would eagerly
seize the boon of pure air and green lanes.
What he really did was to declare an aversion
to a separation from the poor people who had
learned to value his services. Yet, notwithstanding objections, this visitor was taken into
the suburbs, where he also died of fever, after
preaching 'his last best sermon on his dying
bed.' The beneficial influence arising from the
life-work of these toiling evangelists among
the masses cannot well be overrated. The
faithful visitor soon gathers a constituency of
his own. On first entering a district he may
meet with opposition, but in time opposers

learn to respect and even to hold their instructors in affection and honour. What is
better, they learn to make him a confidant,
and will gently complain should he not call
at their rooms sufficiently often.

But it will be well just to refer to the trials
of London city missionaries who visit Jewish
families in this quarter, the annoyances sometimes coming from mere children, whose bigoted
and ignorant parents encourage rudeness in
their offspring. On going his rounds, when
first appointed to a Houndsditch district, one
visitor was followed by numbers of undisciplined
urchins, who seemed to derive peculiar pleasure
from pelting him with rotten fruit, small bags
of flour, and such other missiles as they could
conveniently procure. Because these and other
distractions hindered the work, the man grew
disheartened, and resolved on resigning an office
apparently surpassing human strength; and
an adventure, encountered in a Jewish court,

was not calculated to alter his determination, had nothing happier subsequently occurred. After trying in vain to gain a hearing from a rabble of low Hebrews, the inhabitants of some dirty tenements near at hand, the missionary was leaving amid a volley of abusive epithets, when a lad, seemingly anxious and excited, hastened up and politely inquired if the gentleman would visit a sick woman, who, lying on a bed of weariness, desired instruction and comfort. The missionary readily consented to go, and followed the boy into a forbidding looking house, and up some dark stairs, until coming to a garret, his conductor exclaimed, 'Walk in; you need not knock.' The unwary evangelist entered the room, to find it empty; and when the door closed, and the key turned harshly in the lock, he realised the unpleasantness of being entrapped by a practical joker. The vexation of one in such a position would naturally be overwhelming, and it was not lessened by the unrestrained merriment of the court below. It was a difficult crisis to come out of with safety and dignity. The eager spectators of the street, who at a few minutes' notice had planned this 'lark,' were disappointed when the captive did not stamp, threaten, and call for the police; but as such violent action would have reflected no credit on the London City Mission, their agent adopted a contrary course. Quietly opening the casement, he read in a loud voice, rising in its tones above the clamour below, the fifty-third chapter of Isaiah, and explained how the words prefigured Christ. The tide turned against the jokers; the laugh was defeated, and one was heard confessing to another, 'The fellow *has* pluck!' The fun being over, an amply-bearded German Jew presently appeared at the chamber door and said, 'They have used you shamefully; mind when you go down; they have strewn the stairs with tobacco-pipes.'

Persevering after this, the missionary lived to see the day when he could number twenty-eight avowed converts, besides a hundred Jewish believers in Christ who made no open profession.

While pursuing his arduous calling in such districts, the missionary will necessarily make Saturday the most leisurely day of the week. It is then that, after calling on a few urgent cases of affliction, he will take an excursion into the open country, make up the journal which the rules of the Society require shall be kept, or do a little extra in the way of self-culture. Viewing him thus, as the friend and adviser of a little world, the London City Missionary becomes an object of interest, because we recognise in him a real friend amidst the world of poverty and suffering in which he moves. Most of his constituents well understand the nature of the connection between themselves and the mission, and, accordingly,

value their adviser on account of spiritual
services alone; but the manner in which
others, of less delicate sensitiveness, strive to
turn better things to pecuniary account, is
both perplexing and surprising. While con-
trasting his respectable appearance with their
own too often unprosperous condition, the
people will account the evangelist a well-to-do
gentleman, and push upon him their need of
relief. Nor is all this confined to the indigent.
To-day he may be asked for bread and coal
tickets; to-morrow, a person of too superior a
caste to receive those petty charities, will confidentially request to be accommodated with
£20! Another will want a workshop furnished
with fittings, and knowing no other more
likely friend, he will be obliged by the missionary's signing for the necessary amount!
Others will represent the desirability of his
purchasing certain things which they have to
dispose of; and one has been known to go

so far as to solicit a loan of £5, for providing the *déjeuner* at his daughter's wedding, because he desired to have 'a bit of a flare up.'

But though the most crowded, Petticoat-lane is only one of the many Sabbath morning fairs of London. The 'Lane' and one or two others, such as the bird-market in Spital-fields, have distinguishing traits of their own, but in regard to the rest, to describe one is to describe them all. The air is close and heavily charged with tobacco-smoke and effluvia; the shops have their shutters all down, and their doors are thrown back. The pavement is thronged, while the confusion of voices arising from bawling costermongers, broad-chested butchers, shrill-tongued women, hoarse ballad-mongers, and the deep bass under-current of sound coming from a multi-tude of buyers and sellers, are alone sufficient, so the missionary thinks, to give the unini-tiated visitor nervous fever. There are groups of unwashed men, whose marred faces and slouching mien speak of the previous night's carousal, and of a still inward craving for more fiery stimulants, which cannot be legally supplied until the gin-palaces open at one o'clock. These men are supremely indifferent to what seems to be the reigning confusion. It is home to them—a time of leisure—and they take no active part in the business of the morning beyond passing low jokes to female acquaintances who pass with crying babies and heavily-laden baskets; or perhaps they find additional diversion in kicking some luckless howling cur to the other end of the street, because the animal shows signs of being discomfited by the performance of a blind piper at the corner of a court. The conversation of these idlers is found to be of an unedifying kind, and chiefly relating to prize-fights, tap-room exploits, and divers home adventures and upbraidings in conse-

quence of having 'spent the blunt in lush.'
The whole sight is sufficiently disheartening
if not heart-sickening, and one can scarcely
realise the possibility of gathering from such
a rabble persons who will form a meeting for
the worship of God.

Yet in some regularly appointed room,
slightly secluded from the noisy throng
without, the city missionary sets up, week
by week, on the Sabbath morning, a meeting
for prayer and exhortation. In this hard
service he sometimes accepts the grateful
co-operation of former converts, who volunteer to go round for the purpose of compelling
the people, in the Gospel sense, to come in
and be saved. By such means the low and
the outcast hear the truth, and not unfre-
quently are arrested in a downward course,
ultimately to become new creatures, their
outward reformation being no less striking
than the inward change. Poor women, too,

and not always of the slatternly caste, who
have just finished their morning marketing,
will call at the mission station for a few
minutes, their aprons, meanwhile, being filled
with wares from the baker's, the general
dealer's, and the greengrocer's.   Sometimes
men, half intoxicated, will stumble into the
room, and shed tears, which are too soon
forgotten among degraded associates.   Some
attend for diversion's sake, to find the circumstances of the situation much against
their purpose; and more singular still, the
illiterate Irish will take a timid peep at the
Protestant congregation, and will turn away
in horror because the City Mission provides
neither crosses nor candle-lit altars.

The practice of Sabbath marketing is fraught
with evil to all parties, and in most instances
the shopkeepers would consent to have the
custom abolished by authority.   In one district, notoriously addicted to this desecration

of the day of rest, as many as ninety-seven out of a hundred tradesmen have been known to declare against themselves; and three out of four of a number of shopkeepers who opened on the Sabbath, formerly expressed their desire to enjoy the weekly boon, but because all could not agree, things remained as they were. In such cases legislation would be welcomed as a becoming interference. Both the publicans and the working classes are supposed to have thanked Parliament in their hearts for having closed the public-houses on Sunday morning.

Any who will look into the matter for themselves will find that the chief business in the Sabbath market commences at church time; and is not confined to edibles or wearing apparel, household furniture entering into the category of traffic. At one time a weak effort was made to induce tradesmen to close at eleven o'clock, but this failed entirely;

and now, in many places, Sunday morning is the busiest part of the week; and while the whole of the inhabitants of a district are injuriously affected by a pernicious custom, the chief sufferers are the working people themselves, to whom the practice is supposed to be a convenience. It is well known that the traders charge higher prices, and push the sale of inferior articles, such as they would not venture to sell during the week. Nor are the reasons for this imposition very far-fetched, for extra wages are demanded by the assistants for their seventh-day labours. Some classes of mechanics, from choice rather than necessity, adopt the idle habit of postponing their purchases until the Sabbath, and this being so, it was elicited from several witnesses before a Committee of the House of Commons, some years ago, that the benefits springing from compulsory closing would principally go to the working man; for were not the shops open after Saturday night, the husband would not be so well able to loiter about, smoking and drinking, until too late to provide the weekly stores. 'Suppose she (the wife) could not buy on Sunday, when would she buy?' was asked. 'The husband,' replied the witness, 'would then take care to be at home in sufficient time to have a comfortable dinner on the Sunday.' Even the more respectable Jews declare against the custom, and it breeds contempt for Christianity in Hebrew minds when Christians are found ignoring the claims of conscience. Hebrews themselves risk being discarded by high-principled connections should they carry on business during their own Sabbath.

The individual efforts of missionaries to promote reform against overwhelming opposition are in appearance insignificant, but are not so ineffective as might be inferred from the circumstances of the situation. The visitors frequently succeed in persuading persons to relinquish Sunday business altogether. In the early days of the City Mission, a certain shoe and leather-seller became a striking example of the utility of the gentle persuasions of itinerant evangelists. The warehouse remained open week after week, and regularly, though seemingly without effect, the visitor called, gently to rebuke the sinful custom of the family. The man could not see the influence he was wielding, as little by little the strongholds of the trader's conscience surrendered. The shop was closed, after repeated solicitations and warnings. A daughter was converted at the weekly meeting, and her influence widened until the whole family was Christianized, and until the father died rejoicing in faith.

As I began my sketch with the 'Lane,' the Jews' market, I will add a few lines illustrative of the experience of those who labour among the Scattered Nation.

The poor Jews of London are intensely opposed to the Gospel, and the journals of Christian visitors sent among them abound with records of ill-usage. The missionaries are abused, and even have rubbish thrown at them. This evil arises from other causes than national prejudice. Among the vulgar Hebrews great ignorance exists ; and where ignorance reigns, it matters not whether the subject be Jew or Gentile, passion will bear rule. As a body they are also remiss in educating the young, a failing which sometimes springs from a mercenary spirit—the children's labour being turned to profit.

Many of the lowest class Jews, who live by working for old clothes dealers and such-like employers, exist in a deplorable condition. 'Their dwellings, abounding in vermin, are a mass of filth and corruption,' says one who laboured in a Houndsditch district : 'the sad description of them may be summed up in three words—dirt, emptiness, and wretchedness.'

Of the twenty thousand Jews who reside in London, three-fourths of the number are included in a small radius from Aldgate Church. Popular notions concerning them are often erroneous. They have a thirst for gain, strong and deeply rooted, but their hereditary passion is not gratified so freely as people believe. 'The greater part of them are poor, and much destitution prevails among them,' says a missionary of the Minories. 'Some are often in want of the necessaries of life, and some are scarcely able to obtain a sufficiency to support existence. This is most prominent in the case of the Dutch Jews. Their national charities are numerous and very bountiful, but even they fail to administer sufficient relief.'

Though as a rule even middle-class Jews are not remarkable for cleanliness, they enjoy better average health than Gentiles, and evince a strong taste for fine, showy clothing. Neither are the lowest among them so drunken and so licentious as the ordinary run of vulgar Englishmen, and the women receive a greater amount of respect. As a partial set-off to this honour awarded to the weaker vessel, she is accounted greatly inferior to the man, and too often she is suffered to grow up in blank ignorance; a Hebrew proverb — 'Every one that teacheth his daughter the law is considered as if he taught her transgression'—showing the national sentiment in regard to females. The Jews contemn a woman's testimony, and refuse her a seat with men in the public congregation. In numbers of instances girls are purposely reared in total ignorance, not so much as a knowledge of the alphabet being communicated. Even among men the standard of education is not high, not more than five in every hundred being supposed to know

Hebrew. Both men and women are fond of light amusements, and find much satisfaction at the theatres, as well as at the large taverns where dramatic entertainments are provided.

The advancement of education during the present century has led to a wider expression of opinion; so that while numbers who can judge for themselves reject the superstition of the Talmud and advocate reform, others still adhere to the letter of tradition. While, however, we speak about the spread of knowledge in the Hebrew nation, we may remember that education progresses slowly among a people whose children, on attaining the capacity of earning a shilling a day, are sent to labour rather than to school. But youthful Jews among the poor are not universally neglected, nor does national prejudice entirely exclude them from the benefits of Christian instruction. Their children are taught in Christian Sunday-schools, and, indeed, the Jews themselves have copied our example of opening the Scriptures to youth on the Sabbath, and they also employ religious itinerants to go among the poor and sick of their own persuasion.

The Jews are a sober people, the women being especially circumspect in this respect. 'I cannot charge my memory,' says a visitor in one district, 'with having witnessed a single case of a Jewish woman under the influence of drink.' A partial attempt is made to honour the Sabbath by perpetuating the Mosaical observances; but even the orthodox, who burn two candles on a white cloth during Friday evening, and who refuse to work, will yet descend to many frivolities. The Germans are most easy of access, though their seeming liberality is sometimes rooted in indifference. The Poles and Dutch are reputed to be the most bigoted. 'They know the Bible,' we are told, 'say their prayers in a gabbling way, put on their phylacteries, and curse every one

who does not join in their opinion.' The
Rabbins show little anxiety about spreading
scriptural knowledge among the poor, so that
little can be expected from a people so neglected
more than a piety of formalism. One boy
signified that he should not recognise the Sabbath but for the baked dinner provided for that
day. Then, to other adverse influences which
oppose the endeavours of evangelists, we have
to add the opposition of low Romanists, who
gladly join the Jew in checking the Gospel.
Irish zealots and vindictive Jews have been
known to pelt the Christian visitor beyond the
precincts of their filthy habitations. But the
work has a bright side.

The joy of sincere Jewish seekers after truth
on discovering Christ to be the Messiah is
full and lasting. In Whitechapel stood the
establishment of a photographer, with whom
the district missionary became friendly, but
without seeing any immediate good results.

The artist would not concede that Christ ranked higher than other great historical persons; but being fond of discussion, he one day cautiously introduced an intelligent assistant, and one supposed to be sufficiently versed in Rabbinical lore to confute the Christian argument. This person proved himself an able disputer, and the saloon became the scene of many discussions. Then affairs took an unexpected turn. The assistant, astonished and perplexed at the ground assumed by the Christian, each position being strengthened by quotations from Hebrew Scriptures, exclaimed, 'I wish you had never talked to me. What book is it that teaches you to explain those prophecies which the Rabbins hold as mysteries?' Being told that the book was the New Testament, the reference to Christ provoked harsh language, till in a tone of affected honesty he cried, 'I will read that New Testament, not to believe, but to show you, when I compare it with my books, it is all falsehoods.' These words were acted on; but instead of finding his position impregnable, the inquirer grew bewildered, his features wore a troubled expression, and depressed spirits told of gloom within. The sequel was interesting, and even remarkable. Early one morning there came a knock at the door of the Christian's house, the visitor being the young artist, showing an uneasy manner and a troubled countenance. 'I had a terrible night,'. he cried. 'I could not sleep. I therefore got up, and as I opened the New Testament, my eyes fell on the third of John. I suffer now from the burden of my sins.' Thus this inquirer embraced Christianity, but found he could not do so with impunity. The landlord of the photographer's shop declared he would give his tenant notice to quit if he employed an apostate. What must have been the man's chagrin at hearing the master himself confess the Christian tenets ?

'You may give me notice to leave,' he cried; 'my soul is of more value than all else. I am now quite convinced that Messiah has come, and that He is Jesus, and in Him I hope to believe.' In this manner both master and servant professed themselves sincere converts, through the instrumentality of a city missionary. In Rag Fair, in the New Cut, in Leather-lane, in the bird-market of Spitalfields, and in kindred places, a good and great work is going on, worthy even of the Sabbath morning.

IV.

INFIDELITY IN LONDON.

18 *

IV.

INFIDELITY IN LONDON.

NBELIEF is continually shifting its ground or altering its professions, to suit times and circumstances, and so retain its hold on the age. Deists of the eighteenth century mould are a comparatively rare genus now-a-days, and pure Atheism is not fashionable, because men who wish to appear before others as persons with minds will not lightly embrace the philosophy of fools. Even those weak natures who may have strayed into the uninviting paths of that modified Atheism which is known as

Pantheism, will not be comforted by remembering the aphorism of Mr. Disraeli—'Nothing can be more monstrous than to represent a creator as unconscious of creating.' That horrible and heartlessly cruel lie, which, having an origin in the regions of darkness, gained strength, and stalked abroad in the last century, is becoming in a measure obsolete. Atheism is such an unscientific, boorish sort of belief, that even an artisan with any pretensions to culture and power of mind, will hesitate before avowing among his shopmates that he is only a mere Atheist. The profession carries a degradation with it with which few who have any self-respect care to become associated. It is in fact saying, I am nothing, because I have not the sense to be anything. Thus, in a valuable work* recently published, we read: 'Naked Atheism is a repulsive creed.

* Modern Scepticism. A Course of Lectures delivered at the request of the Christian Evidence Society. Hodder and Stoughton.

It is a heart-withering negation. It touches no sympathy; it stimulates no play of intellect; under the deadly chill of its unlighted vacancy, imagination cannot breathe.'

It appears, then, that in these days even infidelity must not walk abroad clothed in too coarse a habit, unless it would rather disgust than attract votaries. That old beggarly thing, Atheism, in the rags and poverty which presage ultimate decay, may still retain sufficient strength to enounce its absurdities in obscure byeways or in repelling 'halls of science,' but to retain its hold of the more respectable classes, modern unbelief must change both its name and tactics. The contemptible dwarfs who find pleasure in enticing people, more ignorant than themselves, into mere Atheism, will never rise into anything higher than dwarfs — small creatures who account themselves rewarded when complimented on their height by auditors who cannot see.

A striking instance of the manner in which Atheism and its work can bring people to the darkness and misery of dire poverty, occurred some years ago in London. A missionary who was visiting in the neighbourhood of Saffron-hill came to a dilapidated house with a broken door. Knocking, he entered, in response to a weakly-spoken 'Come in,' to find a man and woman living in a condition of shocking wretchedness. Indeed, the spectacle was so utterly horrible that the visitor involuntarily shuddered and sickened at what he saw, familiar as he was with strangely repulsive sights. The man, as an invalid, would have been confined to his bed had he possessed one, but wanting that convenience, he lay on a little straw, beneath a coarse wrapper, with a brick for a pillow! The remainder of the furniture consisted of an old chair and a saucepan. There was no fire, and the woman in attendance, being subject to fits, sat in speechless misery, as if resigned to her fate.

It might have been supposed that such a scene was the result of uncommon profligacy, or that ruin had come from the imprudent and false steps which are taken through ignorance. It was not so, however. The man who lay like a beast in that pestiferous hovel was a gifted author! While in health he had worked for an infidel publisher. He had written poems against Christianity, besides publishing a book to disprove the doctrine of the soul's immortality. A more singular example of the blighting nature of immoral opinions is rarely discovered. When found, such things are worth recording, if only to serve as warnings to others.

At first the sufferer was not disposed to be communicative to the friend who had so unexpectedly invaded a hidden corner in the great City, where a fellow mortal seemingly lay within a few days of death. Yet the two probably understood each other. Perhaps the outcast detected the expression of sympathy on the Christian's countenance; for, as he looked up from his bed of straw, and cast his heavy eyes around the room, he said, 'THIS IS THE WRECK OF INFIDELITY!' A wreck, indeed! His situation was truly dreadful, for poverty and sickness were far from being the only evils borne. The woman in attendance, when maddened by the fits to which she was subject, raged like a hungry tigress, and would spring at her charge with glaring eyes, biting and scratching with the strength of insanity. Then when the fit passed away she became kind and docile.

Of this strange couple the evangelist endeavoured to make friends. The man was highly intelligent, and with a cultured mind prejudiced against the Gospel, it was necessary to begin with the evidences of Christianity.

He listened attentively to the relation of the advent of Christ, and exclaimed, 'Well, that *is* remarkable.' He was then more fully referred to the prophecies pointing to the Messiah, and he said, 'They are quite overwhelming. I do not believe any man can contradict them.' He was spoken to about the Saviour's sufferings, and it was observed that tears ran down the poor infidel's cheeks. He was touched in the heart. His faith in Atheism vanished, though the question of miracles seemed still to be associated with some difficulty. 'Suppose I read the narrative of the Jew who received sight?' said his friend. 'Do, sir, I should like to hear it.' The man listened to the passage and then said, 'That must be true; it carries conviction on the face of it.' He then heard the account of the raising of Lazarus, and on learning how 'Jesus wept,' he interrupted, 'Ah, that was compassion like a God. I cannot help admiring the character of Christ.' The poor fellow became more deeply impressed and was greatly affected. 'I believe now there is a God,' he cried, 'though I have for a long time doubted; but I will never write against Christianity again if I recover. I see such a loveliness in the Christian system, since I have been afflicted, that I begin to love it. Infidelity now appears a cold and heartless thing.' 'Yes,' answers the other, 'it leaves a man to die like a brute. Not so the Gospel of Jesus. No! That blooms with immortality.' Still the man remained for some time in gloom and doubt. He admired prayer, though he could not use it; for after such a course as his, it looked like mocking God. He would have given worlds to appropriate as his own a hymn which was read:—

'Let the sweet hope that Thou art mine,' &c.

He was now frequently found in tears, and on his friend's leaving, he would say, 'When will you come again?' He also confessed,

'My trust in Infidelity is gone. You have no conception of the agony my mind is in. Virtue without Christ is folly.' A dark array of terrors passed through his soul, which gradually subsided as he became enabled to make the coveted gift of prayer his own, and to rejoice in faith. His health was providentially restored. He separated from the woman with whom he had lived in adultery, and returned to his wife and home. After so singular and painful an experience he could well testify, 'Infidelity is an aching void, a blank, a blot, a dark and fearful chasm in which hope sinks, and all that renders life desirable is swallowed up; but religion lights up the gloom, and dispels the dark clouds which hang over human destiny.'

With such facts to enlighten, and with such examples of infatuation to perplex us, we might again ask, What attractions are found in unbelief, and what difficulties are removed by embracing any one of its many systems? Deism, as half obsolete, retains few attractions and may be summarily dismissed. Atheism, or believing in results without a cause, is too gross a folly to be accepted by any beside grovelling, ignorant minds. But is not a pseudo-scientific Pantheism more reasonable? Is there not at least a kind of fascination, a halo of mystery about the idea of 'God in everything'? Happily there is no need in this place to reply to such follies. None of my readers are in any danger of sacrificing their high moral attributes, those endowments which exalt man infinitely above all other creatures of God on earth, and the chief value of which consists in the ability they afford us of taking advantage of the unspeakable privilege of drawing near to Him who is the source of all goodness and of all joy. 'God in everything,' may be a fascinating faith to such as wish in their hearts that there were no God at all.

It may suit the 'intellectual' and the 'cultured' men who have become engrossed in scientific pursuits until they lose sight of the Author of science. These 'advanced' sages may go their way, and the only favour we ask from them is that of being allowed to go ours, since the truest philosophers find it far 'easier to believe in a personal God than in such an impersonal divinity as this Protean force.'

Some few years ago there flourished a certain undertaker in London, who being afflicted with the common disease of *furor loquendi*, made quite a pastime of 'holding forth' in an institution near his home, classically designated the Athenæum. This Athenæum was a rendezvous for infidels of the district, and lectures against Christianity were frequently given. The gifted *savant*, though an undertaker, made some professions of charity and liberality, and also delighted to pass among all men as a person of straightforward integrity. He would doubtless have regarded with high scorn any who supposed that *he* could descend to a mean or underhand subterfuge. But with what inquisitive eyes some people *do* go about. It did not escape the notice of a certain city missionary, also signally gifted in readiness of speech, and who visited thereabout, that this cultured undertaker had caused the device of 'I. H. S.' to be inscribed and borne upon his hearses ! What? Was not this appropriation of a Christian motto a little inconsistent ? The inquisitive missionary decided on going to the Athenæum, thinking he could find something to say bearing on the subject, and something which might benefit a congregation of infidels, though it might fall far short of the soaring intellect of the speaker-in-chief. Accordingly a night was set apart for this purpose of visitation, when the undertaker was found to be lecturing, and lecturing, too, on so original, if not striking, a theme as, 'Found!—a Better Book than the Bible!' Nor was the subject alone remarkable. Some of the able lecturer's remarks were uttered with a profane boldness at which probably some of the less-seasoned frequenters of the Athenæum shuddered, while only listening. He said: 'Jesus Christ never died to save man, and man needs no Saviour, nor is there any truth in Christianity, because so many of its professors are inconsistent.' The inquisitive and ready-tongued city missionary heard these extraordinary utterances, and his tingling ears and heart-swelling indignation appear to have occasioned his sitting uneasily in his chair. The undertaker was evidently mistaken, as all undertakers are liable to become mistaken when they thus neglect their business to handle theological difficulties; and why should not a city missionary, meek Christian though he might be, set even a great tradesman right. He rose in the body of the hall : the eyes of the audience were turned in one direction, curious to see what so humble a creature would do. First, there would of course be a faint cheer; then a good many hisses; all of which were needless, for the intruder wished merely to tell a little story. Had even extreme boldness been needed, that missionary would have been equal to the occasion, for he had spoken of Christ in the more than plague-stricken wards of the Lock Hospital, so that a room filled with infidels could not equal the horrors of the former place. Now, however, he desires to take exception to those words of the undertaker just quoted, *e. g.:* ‘At the time of the French Revolution the leaders adopted the motto, “ Death is an eternal sleep.” This motto they placed over their public buildings, their churches, and their tombs. Now, if I as *a Christian-teacher* had gone to France at that time, and adopted the Atheistical motto, and placed it over my door for the sake of getting into favour with the infidels, what would you have thought of me?' This was a straightforward appeal to manly self-respect, and as such was easily comprehended by the cultured intellects of the Athenæum. 'What punishment would have been deserved under such circumstances as those described?' The response came ringing from all parts of the hall, 'You ought to have been scouted.' An advantage was undoubtedly gained when the people answered just as the speaker desired. But what of that? All frequenters of the Athenæum were safe enough. When or where were Free-thinkers ever found dealing in such double-faced humbug as corresponded to that French Revolution illustration? Very good. And now Mr. Missionary has something further to say. 'You are all very right: I ought. But your lecturer is guilty of precisely such a crime! *He* has adopted the Christian's motto, "I. H. S.," which means, "Jesus the Saviour of men;" and he has put this motto on his Gothic hearses. Now let him first go home and pull off that motto, before he comes here to find fault with Christians for *their* inconsistency with their principles; for as long as he has that motto on his hearses you must necessarily regard him as himself an inconsistent man.' The able undertaker did not go to the Athenæum in any way prepared for this surprising turning of the tables. The hubbub of confusion which ensued, however, may at least have supplied an excuse for his remaining silent.

But our friend had not yet done with diverting adventures. The Christian missionary, who thus presumed to baffle a public character, seemed ever to stand in the way, ready to spoil the effects of that public character's best efforts. The paltry affair of merely placing religious devices on hearses might soon be forgotten, were that all. It was not all! This missionary's memory, joined to the fund of illustration he possessed, made his presence even more than undesirable. It was absolutely annoying. But men of knowledge and influence must hold on their way and preserve their temper. The under-taker won a living among Christians, so that it would, perhaps, suit his policy not to be too hard. He would still lecture, but it should next be on the more. liberal subject of 'The Benevolence of those who have rejected Christianity.' Benevolence among Atheists? Yes; though a man be an unbeliever, and even an unbelieving undertaker, it is pleasant to pass through the world as a genial and large-hearted fellow. The lecture was delivered, and scarcely had the cheers of an admiring audience died away, than that ubiquitous meddlesome city missionary was, as usual, on his legs. What! Another story? Yes, Mr. Missionary had another story to tell, a very

seasonable one, too, for it was illustrative of
'The benevolence shown by men who have
rejected Christianity.' He said: 'A poor
family lost several of their children in-succes-
sion by scarlet fever, which occasioned them
great pecuniary distress. At their request I
waited on the undertaker they employed, to
beg of him to reduce his charges on the last
interment, on account of their distress. He
was out. I saw his wife, but she positively
refused to do so, and would not abate one
penny. I had therefore to raise the money
among my friends who professed Christianity.
But the undertaker was an infidel.' Shouts
of 'Name!' from the indignant auditors
were now heard. 'Shall I tell you the name
of the man?' continued the speaker. The
only reply was 'Name!' 'That man,'
replied the missionary, finishing his speech,
'that man was your lecturer, and this is the
practical confirmation of what he has been

telling you.' Thus the good work of the itinerant evangelist proceeds. It is a warfare both offensive and defensive, and great victories are not wanting.

In these infidel lecture-rooms the agents of the City Mission do more than speak: they distribute hundreds of tracts and handbills on the fallacies of infidelity. With few exceptions these are taken by the men, though occasionally the spirit of unbelief is shown, when the distributors of the little messengers have their papers thrown back to them. Or a venturesome Atheist may perhaps offer to dispute on a given evening; and then, when actually pressed to do so, will find that he has miscalculated his strength, and so makes a timely retreat. On one evening, a man, whose hairs were become grey in a bad service, rose to give an account of an experiment tried by a certain surgeon, who, sympathising with the advanced liberalism, magnanimously devoted a few spare hours of his valuable time to the furtherance of 'science.' This enlightened surgeon minutely examined the brains of several dead persons, in order to discover traces of mind! His researches were completely unsuccessful, and therefore was it not plain, to any but the most unreasonable and prejudiced, that mind or spirit becomes extinct at death? Now, an argument so curiously original against the doctrine of the soul's immortality, might have passed current with customary honours had it not been for a circumstance perhaps unforeseen on the part of the speaker. That same meddlesome and talkative evangelist, who had ventured even to rebuke a literary undertaker, happened to be present, and, as might have been expected, he neutralised the intended effect of the last speaker's words, appropriating as his own what fun the discussion afforded. 'Your surgeon,' he said, 'was as great a fool as the boy who cut the bellows open to see where the wind came from; and one experiment proves as much as the other!'

Secularism was started in London some years ago, and probably this specious system has been more readily embraced than some others by persons who have received religious training and have backslidden from early teaching. Secularism would seem to be a middle way, into which the doubting are invited to walk. It does not shock people's finer instincts, like Atheism, and has not so many subtle turns to exercise and perplex feeble intellects, as Pantheism. Its leading doctrine is,—make the most of this life, eat, drink, and enjoy yourself, for you know nothing about any other state beyond the present world. In fact, Secularism is a short-life-and-a-merry-one kind of creed, and one such as is likely to be embraced by those who are ready to accept any secondhand belief which grants them license to indulge in sensual gratification. It professes to make the most of life; but probably not a few, by embracing its principles, have made the worst possible use of this world, even in pecuniary matters.

Many who read these lines may perhaps remember the dingy little dépôt in Fleet-street, whence, during some years, the publications of Sècularism emanated, and which, happily, in course of time, was necessarily closed. The organ of the system, *The Reasoner*, was issued weekly at a penny, and was then started as a full-priced weekly newspaper, until, through lack of support, its publication was discontinued, the office being now occupied by ordinary publishers. All right-thinking Christians must regret that men like some of the leading exponents of Secularism — men whose knowledge and abilities eminently fit them to act as the friends and the guides of the working classes — should seek to satisfy the cravings of their higher nature by straying into the uninviting ways of this already effete system. Yet while thoroughly assured that the ethics of the Secularist can never satisfy those whom they delude, we should in justice distinguish between them and the rampant blasphemy and coarse democracy of certain Atheistical fanatics, who unfortunately have ready access to the ears of large numbers of the working classes. The more moderate system is destructive to the soul, in common with its horrible competitor, but it is not so disgustingly repelling to decent people.

Secularism accepts and appropriates much of the morality of the Bible. It will introduce many of the sacred precepts into its every-day life, though it rejects all notions of inspiration, disbelieves in a future state, and without wishing directly to acknowledge the humiliating fact, the creed appears before us as Deism re-habited and re-named. Though it preaches liberality, theory and practice do not always harmonise even with Secularists. All classes of unbelievers, and especially such as are deficient in knowledge, are intolerant towards others, and impatient under contradiction. How else can we account for the frightful blasphemy and insanely violent language too frequently heard in 'Halls of Science'? Freedom of opinion and of discussion? What does it mean when pleaded for by men who become enraged if a wife be found reading a Christian book, or infusing into her children's minds the life-lessons of the Bible?

The more persons become familiar with Infidelity as it really is, the less will they incline to a belief in the heart-sincerity of those who embrace any one set of the conflicting tenets. In the majority of instances, we may fear that poorly educated persons imbibe the sentiments of leading authors of the sceptical school, and then, in pride or obstinacy, defend them in .very desperation. It is well, nevertheless, that conscience often capitulates when hard pressed. The faintest spark of a love of something better may sometimes be fanned into a living flame if the proper means be used.

One evening a man, who resided in Southwark, attended a missionary's meeting for the special purpose of lauding Paine and Voltaire as writers whose moral sentiments surpassed in beauty anything of the kind found in the Bible. What this objector to the Gospel had to say was listened to with deference, and then he was asked if ever he had read the volume he contemned. Yes, he had read the Bible, in common with other books. 'Have you a family?' asked the missionary who was presiding over the little assembly. Yes, the speaker possessed a wife and little ones. Which, then, would he recommend to *them,* —the life-companion who was dear to him and the children whom he loved—Infidelity or Christianity? The company may have looked curiously to see what shape the infidel's answer would assume, but they could little have suspected what its import would be. What was their astonishment when the champion of unbelief, of a few minutes before, burst into tears, and then cried, '*I never heard that kind of argument before. I would rather give them the Bible than any infidel book.*' Such are the victories of kindness and patience which hard-working evangelists achieve in their daily work.

The manner in which infidels are taken, as it were, in their own meshes, by skilful disputants, would form both an instructive and piquant chapter in the annals of street evangelisation. Some years ago there lived

in London two boorish shoemakers, who were
commonly found pursuing their craft on Sabbath mornings. Besides being avowed infidels,
they sympathised with Republicans and Char-
tists, meanwhile stoutly maintaining that the
Bible hindered the progress of mankind.
Would nobody volunteer to go and tell these
desperadoes of their errors and duty? It was
scarce to be expected that genteel church-goers
could think, even, of turning aside from their
pathway of respectability to do anything so unfashionable. Talk of the Gospel to unwashed
cobblers on a Sabbath morning? Impossible!
Then in regard to the city missionary; he had
been warned by a friendly voice not to venture
near so notorious a den as the shoemakers'
room. Why? The men were sheer heathens,
and probably dangerous. Yet, notwithstanding
these kind warnings, the evangelist ventured
into the forbidden precincts, and on entering
the apartment he was not directly insulted.

On the contrary, he met with a negative sort of civility by being allowed to stand for some time unnoticed. As it would have been un-wise to have begun at once about religion, a conversation respecting America was first introduced. The speaker, having once lived in the New World, remembered having worn, pegged boots there. Ay, to be sure, America was the place for good workmen. 'I wish I had gone ten years ago,' said one of the men, though in rather ungracious tones. An advance in the right direction was made when the visitor referred to the great numbers of places of worship with which America abounded. 'It may be all the worse for that,' growled one of the men. 'I am sorry to hear you speak so,' was the reply. 'You know the Scriptures assure us that righteousness exalteth a na-tion.' This remark provoked quite a fierce explosion of wrath. 'I don't mind what the Bible says. . . People who talk most about religion are the greatest liars, and they are the hardest men I ever worked for.' 'Ay, that they are,' put in the other man, who hitherto had remained silent. From the conversation which now followed, it appeared that the first speaker, like so many ill-informed objectors to the claims of religion, had never read the pages of Inspiration he so vehemently denounced. On being driven into a corner in the argument, he could say nothing more effective than, 'I have read quite enough of it.' In truly commendable good temper and moderation the missionary replied, 'That is not the open answer I expected from you.' You have declared the Bible to be false and foolish : have you come to that awful conclusion after close and diligent study?' 'Indeed, I have other things to study,' cried the shoemaker, impatient over this interruption to their morning's labour. 'I don't want to know anything about it —I am busy just now.' One might turn from such a place, and from such a man when in a bad temper, heart-sick and despairing; might almost conscientiously resign such to their fate as incorrigible, or say something hastily which might provoke them beyond reclamation. Only by special tact, blessed by heaven, can seeds of truth be sown in this not always sterile soil of unbelief. The visitor continued: 'You appear to be a hard-working man, and to possess some knowledge of your line of business. Now, about ten days ago, I purchased a pair of shoes for eight shillings and sixpence. Do you think I gave too much for them?' 'No, if they were a good pair,' said the man. 'Do you think them a good pair?' enquired the other, emphatically. 'Show them to me, and I'll soon tell you.' 'They are at home,' still answered the other. 'Cannot you tell me whether they are good or bad, without seeing them?' 'None but a fool would ask such a question,' said the man. Not ask

such a question ? Why not ? Here was surely
a very unaccountable circumstance. A crafts-
man, thoroughly initiated into the mysteries of
a certain trade, confesses inability to judge
whether articles are good or indifferent without
first handling and testing them. In the mean
time a book, which likewise he has never read
or examined, he unhesitatingly pronounces to
be an imposture. 'I am but a stranger,' now
said the visitor, 'yet I cannot forbear telling
you that the Scriptures have given *me* great
peace, and I sincerely desire your peace and
happiness. This has brought me to your house,
and has kept me waiting here for nearly an
hour, and this it was that made me pass by
your long ungracious silence after I entered
your room.' Now, even shoemakers love victory
in argument; but here one was unmistakably
defeated. All that men can do in such circumstances, is to retail a few threadbare objections
to Christianity, and make a show of intel-

ligently comprehending what they profess to believe. It is likewise very galling to be silenced before fellow-workmen. 'I'll tell you what,' cried the man, who all through had maintained the argument, 'had you come in preaching and canting, I would have chucked you through that door.' Clearly perceiving his defeat, however, he was in no mood for continuing hostilities. In a surprising manner he gracefully surrendered the position. He even rose from his seat to offer the visitor a chair, and probably for the first time in his life listened attentively to the Gospel. That man in time became a real convert, a devoted Christian, and a diligent student of Scripture. While such things are occurring, shall we not take courage? How many gems may be won for the seeking. How many souls, living on husks, and shivering in rags of their own patch-work, might wear the wedding robe and sit in their Lord's banqueting-house, were the messengers abroad only to compel them to come in.

Possibly some unbeliever may scan these lines. To such I say, do not rest satisfied with merely doubting Christianity. *Be sure you are right.* Weigh the best things of your system against the Christian's peace and hope, and deal honestly with your own heart. Test a question with such tremendous issues free from the prejudice which perhaps you have taken second-hand from infidel writers and lecturers. Test your principles before death comes to test them for you! Be sure you are right!

V.

LONDON ROUGHS.

V.

LONDON ROUGHS.

ON all hands in our vast and little-understood London we find examples of the human genus with characters indigenous to their various districts. 'You knows I believe what you say,' said one of the rarer species, in docile ignorance, addressing a missionary; 'but you know the likes of us, that never had any larning, who have always been travelling the country ever since we was born, it aren't to be thought that we could know much about these things. My

father was a great drunkard all his life; he
could earn plenty of money, but he used to
spend it as fast as he earned it. I was born
on the road, as we was travelling—at least,
so my mother tells me, poor old girl! but
she has been dead for years. From a boy
I always travelled with my father. Warn't I
frightened once! Why my old dead father
said to me once as we was near a wood, "I
say, boy, I have often said I will never die
with my shoes on;" so he climbed up a tree—
I at the same time crying to him not to do
it, for I was quite a boy, about twelve years
old. He got up a tree, chucked me down his
shoes, and says, "Here goes, boy!" and hung
himself with his neck-handkerchief. I ran to
a man close by in the road, filling a cart, and
told him my father had hung himself, and
asked him to come and cut him down; but
he would not, saying he warn't going to cut
him down if he was fool enough to hang

himself. So I ran crying, and met two gentlemen in the road. They came just in time to
save my poor old father's life; but he was
ill a long time, and at last he died raving
mad through drink a few years after. I go
to church sometimes; but you knows the par-
sons are so learned, that such poor ignorant
creatures as us cannot understand them. We
can understand all *you* say, because you make
it so plain to us; and when we come home
my old woman gets the Book and reads it
all over to me again.' This man and his wife
seemed to derive much pleasure and profit
from the Sabbath evening meetings, and gave
satisfactory evidence of having undergone the
saving change. 'We see,' said this itinerant
tinker, 'that none but Jesus Christ can save
such poor sinners as we are.'

Strangers settling in London, as well as
older residents, will do well to learn that it
is not always safe to trust the testimony of

eyes and ears. What is seen and heard may need explaining, and few interpreters of the manners and customs of the poor surpass our city missionaries. Ordinary passengers see numbers who flaunt abroad a specious poverty, while they fare only too abundantly: the visitor of a poor district can tell of numbers who, though scorning to solicit alms, are pinched by bitter poverty.

There once lived a certain lady in London, who, being of an artless nature, was kind and sympathising, ever ready to lighten another's burden and to show kindness to the afflicted. Near her house a crossing was kept by one who fattened on the kindness of his neighbours, and seemed not only to accept as a right such coins as were dropped into his capacious hat, but also many left-off garments of gentlemen who walked over the cleanly-swept roadway. But there is no need for exercising unceasing industry, even on the part of crossing-sweepers, provided they have ordinary ingenuity. Say, a charitably disposed lady lives at No. ———. Very well. She has the reputation of being peculiarly liberal to persons laid aside by sickness. So far all is very good. If you cannot make yourself ill, or do not care to tamper with your constitution, a feigning of indisposition will still serve your purpose. So, at least, appears to have reasoned our intelligent crossing-sweeper. The roadway was forsaken; the man of the broom lay up comfortably, and giving out that he was 'very bad,' probably also taught his wife to shake her head and look as miserable as a woman should do in immediate prospect of widowhood. The notice of the lady was soon attracted; and, what was of more moment, the crossing-sweeper's humble larder was speedily replenished with many good things which he knew the visitor was not backward in dispensing. But why stop short at mere sickness?

A benefactor who will supply half-crowns, mutton-chops, wine, and preserves, merely because one suffers from influenza or a liver affection, would behave even more handsomely in defraying the expenses of a worthy body's funeral. So, again, as it would seem, reasoned the keen-witted genius of the crossing. Ignorant of the proverb which warns the living against personating the great enemy, he boldly resolved on feigning death; and, as he opined, the lady of No. —— soon appeared at the house of mourning, with sympathy expressed even in her nod and step. The usual concomitants of death were visible—the darkened room, the bedstead, bearing the remains of the loved one, neatly covered with a sheet, and the 'widow,' with a sombre cast of countenance, treading lightly, as though fearful of disturbing her husband's repose. Then there would be the half-whispered thanks, and recitals of the manner in which the last hours of the deceased were cheered by the half-crowns, the mutton-chops, wine, and preserves, so considerately contributed. But one heavy consideration remained. How could she, a lone woman, raise funds for becomingly interring such a husband? Should she have recourse to the parish? Abhorrent thought to a woman of self-respect and feeling! *Her* husband, indeed, should never be carried to the grave like a pauper! The lady from No. ——, in her artlessness, did not look very closely into matters, and never suspected the reality of what she saw, nor the truth of what she heard. Moved by pity, she went straightway from the crossing-sweeper's lodging to make a collecting tour among some friends, who, appreciating these efforts to relieve deserving poverty, subscribed sufficient for providing a decent funeral. The money was carried to the tearfully grateful widow, and was doubtless accompanied by suitable words of counsel and

Christian consolation. How grateful would be the emotions of such a philanthropist while retracing her homeward way! Doing good brings its own reward! Deserving poverty must be searched after! The lady had not progressed far, however, when she discovered the loss of a glove. She returned, and, there being no necessity for ceremony, abruptly entered the apartment she had left but a few minutes before. Judge of her sensations when the ' corpse ' appeared sitting up on the bed, conversing with the ' widow ' in a very earthly fashion; and, as it also seemed, well satisfied with the net gains of the 'dying' scheme, though a little discomposed at the unbecoming reappearance of the lady from No. ———. This man's brazen-faced impudence enabled him to return to his crossing; but he subsequently became influenced for good by the London City Mission.

Striking and valuable as a revelation into

the character of the roughs was the experience
of a missionary on the eve of the execution
of the murderer Mullens, some years ago. The
case exciting universal interest, the night prior
to the final tragedy saw the taverns around
Newgate crowded with the lowest of the populace; and when these houses closed for the
night, half-drunken men and women, as one
vast, blaspheming, noisily obscene rabble, occupied the ground before Newgate, to await the
final spectacle. Being abroad on his district
on that evening, a missionary entered a public-
house near the prison; but before leaving the
bar Mr. Landlord honestly warned him that
on such an occasion, when the ruffianism of
London inundated the vicinity, it would con-
stitute mere wanton rashness to court insult
among the company of the taproom. Deaf to
these good-natured cautions, the visitor unhesitatingly proceeded to the dreaded apartment,
where, in an atmosphere thick with fumes of

spirits and tobacco, a hardened company were joking, scoffing, swearing, and conversing in general about the murderer and the murdered. The stranger's entrance produced a marked sensation. There were immediate cries of 'Bonnet him,' 'Kick him out,' &c., while one gentleman called to the waiter, 'Bring a quartern of gin and two outs (glasses), for me and this chap to drink Mullens' health.' But the villanous crew little suspected the quality of the human metal they were dealing with, or misapprehended the strength of character by which they would easily be checkmated. First they thought to frighten the intruder by closing around the door to prevent his escaping; but instead of sudden flight he called out in a loud, clear voice, 'If a thousand savages were here I'd have my say out; and do you think I am to be cowed by sixty or seventy Englishmen? Why, I have come to tell you of the last dying speech of a Friend who was executed.' These words were effective, for silence was immediately demanded in such peremptory terms as ' Muzzle,' ' Hold yer mug,' ' Shut up,' &c. Then followed the great history —Once upon a time, many centuries ago, two notorious malefactors were condemned to execution; and then, as now, throngs of spectators entered the city to witness their death. But one greater than a creature, the God-man, who had done no wrong, voluntarily laid aside His glory to redeem the guilty. He was also condemned to crucifixion, and on His cross our sins were nailed. Some unseen angel might have inspired with reverence this wildly wicked company, so eagerly and silently did they listen to the relation of the heavens darkening, the rocks being rent, and how earth quaked. The whole spectacle presented at Calvary was described; and on the speaker's coming to the last scene, and repeating the words of Christ, ' It is finished,' pipes were laid down all round the room, and wonder sat on many a countenance. No resistance being now offered to the missionary's leaving, numbers rose in respect as he passed, and two men, who followed him into the street, promised in God's strength to forsake their wicked course. From such examples of Christian bravery we learn to appreciate the Gospel's irresistible, all-conquering power.

Some of the characters classed as roughs are so notoriously iniquitous that they become a source of terror and amazement to such as are themselves of sufficiently low morals. Yet even these are sometimes highly susceptible of truth, which once having entered their hearts, they hold with a tenacity not always shown by persons who have enjoyed higher privileges.

It is touching to discover what kind of characters fraternise at the little gatherings known as the missionary's meetings. 'Did you know that you lately had at your meeting one who had been in chains at Newgate under sentence of death?' 'Have *you* been in that melancholy situation?' was enquired. 'I have; and your simple remarks affected me very much as you spoke of prisons and what you had seen in them.' This subject, after serving at Portsmouth, became a ragged-school teacher.

Notwithstanding their ignorance and blunted instinct, even the roughs of a district foster attachment for those who live for their welfare. When one indefatigable missionary was accidentally killed some years ago on the London and North Western-Railway, his unlettered constituency showed deep concern for the loss sustained. On the day of the funeral the shops of the vicinity — many of them not ranking above coal-sheds and cats'-meat establishments —were half closed, and groups at street corners bewailed the general bereavement. 'God help me! What shall I do now Mr. Miller is gone?' cried an Irishwoman in tears. 'He was always at me about the drink, and I thought at one time he would make a good job of me.' A crowd followed the cortege as far as Waterloo Bridge, and numbers. being too poor to pay the toll, turned back weeping. 'Ah,' cried an invalid in St. Saviour's and Christ Church Union, 'you don't know how great our loss is. If God's people lose their pastor they can *go* to another; but Mr. Miller *came* to us.' The Mr. Miller mentioned as having been accidentally killed, was returning home with a small party, and at the moment of the fatal collision they were singing the Evening Hymn.

Christian England is doubtless making praiseworthy efforts in the work of evangelisation, but perhaps not according to her ability. Would that our fathers had shown more solicitude for the good of perishing thousands; for it is painful to reflect how one generation after another has passed from the fetid courts and alleys of London without having the Gospel

carried among them. Then evidence continually comes to the surface of the gratitude of
those who receive benefit. Testimonials have
repeatedly been presented to missionaries; and
one case happened of a laundress, who, as-
cribing conversion to this agency, insisted on
acting as unpaid nurse when the missionary of
her district was seized with cholera. Another
pleasing sign is the eagerness after knowledge
shown by persons coming under Christian influence—persons who otherwise would continue
coarse and repelling.

A wood-chopper of Bethnal-green, who bore
an indifferent name, thus answered a first
Christian appeal: 'Perhaps, after all, you are
right. I never learned a letter in my life, and
so can't judge. I'm told the Bible is a pack
of lies; and here's one to begin with. It says
a man gave five hundred hungry men as much
as they could eat out of five loaves and two
fishes. Why, if they wasn't as big as a house,

there wouldn't have been a bit apiece. I believe
it's all a lie, I do.'   He listened to the true
account and its explanation — that Christ, the
Son of God, fed not five hundred, but five
thousand, as described in the Gospel.   The
man at once did homage to truth. 'What a
blessing it is to know the right thing!' he
said. 'I have lived all these years, and know
nothing.   Nobody never took no trouble to
learn me nothing when I was a boy. I wish
I had been a scholar; I shouldn't act as I do.
I should like to read this here Bible, particular
about Him you was speaking about; but there,
nobody won't take no notice of such as me, and
I hangs about anywhere.'   Thousands of such
subjects as this old wood-chopper are waiting
to have the Gospel carried to them, and to be
gathered into the Church.

Hard-working missionaries learn not to limit
the power of God. Were they for a moment
to lose confidence in the invisible power sus-

taining the good cause and strewing the path of the faithful with blessing, they would lose ground, disheartened. Prejudice, bigotry, hard-heartedness, and ignorance have to be overcome; but happily the conquest belongs to God. A man might as well hope to splinter a mass of granite with his fist as to subdue by human means the stony heart. But faith and persevering labour are constantly working miracles.

In a squalid room in a low district flourished a cobbler, of whom the neighbours heard little, excepting when family brawls brought him under prominent notice. The offspring partook of their parents' nature. A son was already dead, having been driven mad by drunkenness. The wife of another son, finding it impossible to live with her husband, had left her home, while the only daughter lived a life of shame. When he first sought admission at the door of the attic wherein the old shoemaker and four others herded, the missionary might well have retreated in disgust, and have asked himself if venturing thither was not merely exposing holy things to ridicule. To make the first impression more lasting, if less favourable, two pigs were vehemently demanding a meal in one corner, while a dog roamed over the room in frolicsome playfulness. In this home, however, the Gospel wrought amazing changes, the more surprising as none of the family were able to read. The room became clean and orderly; peace succeeded brawling; and the wife by her altered walk and conversation won the sobriquet of The Lady. These results are the best rewards for toiling workers. Every such triumph stamps their message as Divine. Another couple were encountered whose quarrels astonished when they did not terrify beholders. The man and his wife fought like wild animals when intoxicated, and vied each with the other in demolishing the household furniture, for while the woman would destroy a window-pane, the more competent masculine fist would shatter a looking-glass. Then each would seize a chair, and each would excite the other's rage by the readiness with which they converted furniture into firewood. Such are the roughs among whom the Gospel is promoting civilisation. There is one sad reflection in connection with this subject: when men and women become thus utterly depraved, the women are the more repulsive. Nor is this merely an opinion. In the refractory wards of workhouses a missionary has been received civilly by men, while women have assailed him with abuse and obscenity.

The danger or injury to which our itinerants are exposed is well known. On opening the door of a room in a west-end district, in response to a welcome of 'Come in,' there appeared a company of Irish carousing over a can of beer. Supposing them to be half intoxicated, the visitor judged it unadvisable to do more than lay some tracts on the table and speak a few passing words; but as he retired, a powerful fellow obstructed the doorway, and called out with an oath, 'No going out of this room until you have paid your footing.' The company rose, and amid noise and confusion commenced pulling the intruder hither and thither, trying to make him drink, till a woman, whose bonnet had just been pawned to supply the liquor, interfered. 'You'll frighten the man; he has not been used to such treatment.' 'Frighten!' replied the prisoner, with seeming unconcern; 'do not I know what Irish are too well to be frightened at them?' At these words peace was immediately proclaimed, and they listened for an hour to instruction and exhortation.

It is pleasing to find how highly the missionaries rank in the affection even of rough characters. Vicious and dishonest people abound who would not bemean themselves by offering insult to the messengers of Christ. *They* at least may walk infamous districts without molestation. Many seemingly trivial occurrences have shown how deeply rooted in man is a reverence for what he knows to be right. A St. Giles's visitor has lost a handkerchief, to have it returned with apologies as taken by a 'new-comer.' Another 'new-comer' attempted a like robbery in a court, when he was immediately surrounded by other thieves, and made to render polite reparation.

These things are good so far as they go; but still more grateful is the simple faith of the 'rough' species on their first taking to religion. Some of us have scant sympathy with a modern fashion which raises men once eminent for wickedness into responsible Christian teachers. It is probably better that ex-thieves, ex-pugilists, and ex-roughs in general should forbear intruding into the pulpit, since religion gains more by their good example in private life than by their assumption of public stations.

A concluding reminiscence may be given relating to the rather novel experience of three missionaries, who a few years ago endeavoured to impart religious instruction to the most renowned of modern prize-fighters. In connection with one celebrated combat, this man and his prowess for the moment were a leading theme of popular conversation, and his gains, including many presentations, appear to have amounted to a small fortune. The ignorance of this pugilist was deplorable; but possessing enough native shrewdness to see that his own profession clashed with the principles of Christianity, he for long refused to tolerate 'a parson.' Robust as was his constitution, and singularly great as was his muscular power, disease early sapped his vigour, and he was laid aside in helpless weakness. Hearing of his illness, the first missionary sought admission to the house, without success. The second was more fortunate; for, visiting the 'champion,' he read and prayed with him, and left some little volumes, but when the patient partially recovered, the good impression seemed to wear away. Then came a relapse, and a third missionary regularly attended him until death. The poor fellow in his last illness showed no reluctance to receive Christian counsel; on the contrary, he valued the services rendered, and several times sent specially for his instructor. Interesting, if not remarkable, were the events of the last day of this man's life. When symptoms of speedy dissolution appeared, a cab was despatched in haste after the missionary, and approaching the bedside of the dying man, he read the chapter containing the words, 'This is a faithful saying and worthy of all acceptation, that Christ Jesus came into the world to save sinners, of whom I am chief.' The last clause was caught up by the pugilist, and he faintly repeated, '*Of whom I am chief.*' The tear of pity may fall, but charity hopeth all things. Poor ——, he confessed that drink had involved him in ruin and death. Then he at least honoured the Gospel by separating from the woman with whom he had been living in adultery. Unhappily, of any further progress of grace in his heart we cannot speak. We may nevertheless rejoice that he and such as he are not allowed to pass from mortality without hearing of that Divine mercy which, making no distinction among sinners, calls on all in common to take their iniquity to the cross of Christ—to believe and live.

PART II.—EDINBURGH.

Burns.

I.

A DAY WITH THE MEDICAL MISSION.

A DAY WITH THE MEDICAL MISSION.

ERSONS who need rest from labour, either mental or physical, can always secure a profitable change by arranging for a temporary sojourn in

'Edina, Scotia's darling seat.'

The pride of Scotland, Edinburgh, will continue to maintain her prestige while travellers are found who appreciate cultured society, historical relics, and a highly romantic natural situation. The city possesses every gratification to allure and detain educated visitors.

17 *

Nature enters into an alliance with literature, science, and art, to render the city favoured and famous.

Observant English visitors who walk out into Edinburgh for the first time notice what a different aspect the town presents from some other capitals with which they are familiar. There is a classical and refined look about the New Town, with its gardens, Scott's monument, museum, and picture gallery, quite unique and striking, and which can never be seen in great commercial centres. The pedestrians, the young women not excepted, include a large proportion of students, and carry a literary air. Even the shopkeepers look studentish, and in many instances are persons of respectable attainments. Then how thickly strewn are the relics of the past on this famous historical site — from the ancient little chapel, wherein 'good Queen Margaret' prayed, on the top of Castle-rock, to the now dilapidated pulpit of John Knox, or the murderous Grass Market 'Maiden' in the Antiquarian Museum. Dr. Guthrie thinks that, with the exception of some parts of Old Paris, Europe does not contain a more interesting place than Old Edinburgh.

An inquisitive visitor who passes along the now squalid, but once important, thoroughfare of the Cowgate, towards the Grass Market, will be sure to have his eye attracted by a quaint and slightly decayed building, dating from the sixteenth century, and ornamented with a spire in the centre. Over the entrance is an inscription, ' HE THAT HATH PITIE VPON THE POOR LENDETH UNTO THE LORD, AND THE LORD WILL RECOMPENSE HIM THAT HE HETH GIVEN.' In addition to the motto from the Book of Proverbs, may be noticed the arms of the Guild of Hammermen, keeping company with the crest of the founder of what was in old time an hospital, Michael Macquhan. The chapel and the buildings attached, now standing in the very worst part of the Cowgate, have long, long since parted with their ' praying men' and monkish associations, and are now the chief dispensary of the Edinburgh Medical Mission.

The premises pointed out will amply repay inspection, in consequence of their being a curious and well-preserved relic of pre-Reformation times. In the coloured window of the chapel are seen the arms of the founder of the house, with those of Mary of Guise. In the centre of the room, beneath what is now the pulpit, with its marvellously-carved high-backed chair, is the identical table on which the corpse of Argyll was laid after execution, on the last day of June, 1685. Within this same building, so little altered by time since the most stirring days of Scottish history, John Craig, the contemporary and assistant of Knox, preached in Latin after his return from exile. Here, too, tradition says, the first General Assembly of the Church of Scotland was convened.

This hospital having much in common with the ordinary monastery, was established in the sixteenth century, and was intended for the 'Sustentation of several poor men who should continually there put forth their prayers to Almighty God.' When once founded, 'the Crosse House' had its endowments from time to time augmented by pious donors, whose supplementary gifts to the charity of Michael Macquhan are carefully chronicled in the panelling of the chapel. The ancient table, antique chair, the now rusty sword, formerly used on state occasions, and all the other furniture of this Magdalen Hospital, seem to bid us linger and learn what they can tell us of the past; but perhaps a still more interesting object is the tomb of Dame Macquhan, the founder's wife, which bears the inscription, 'Here lyes ane honorabil woman, Janet Rhynd, ye spous of umquhil Micel Makquhan, burges of Edinburgh, founder of yis place, and decessit ye

iii^d day of December, A.D. 1553.' Such is the
home of a mission which seeks to relieve suffering in its severest form, and to teach the ignorant the way of salvation. Let us follow its
agents to their work, and see in what their
labours consist.

To see the Medical Mission in actual opera-
tion, I repair to the Cowgate on a week-day at
two p.m., when the patients congregate in an
apartment used on Sabbath evenings for the
Ragged School. If we enter the room now that
service has just begun, we shall find a motley
group of characters, each having some bodily
affliction, or acting as the messenger of others
whose weakness prevents personal attendance,
or lending assistance to those too weak to
reach the place alone. The middle-aged man
with wasted cheeks and deep sepulchral cough
sits by the side of ailing youth, or the dame
whose addiction to whiskey has occasioned her
being injured in a nocturnal brawl. The dis-

tressed mother sits there, keeping close to her afflicted child—both looking worthy objects for the advice and medicine here bestowed. The room is well filled, and the congregation, though a small one, presents an uncommon picture of patient and impatient suffering. These people have bodies to be healed; but, while giving them the best service they are able, those in office never forget that they are Christian teachers as well as medical practitioners. Happily, our friends know their art and understand their opportunities. They know that persons benefited physically are almost certain to open their hearts to receive religious teaching. Moreover, many in the room are Romanists, who would surely shun these precincts were no advice or medicine forthcoming. Better rot and die in squalid ignorance than be raised to respectability at the expense of imbibing Protestant teaching! So think some of the savagely bigoted teachers of these poor

Irish—teachers who also say that there is less
sin incurred in shooting a man than in eating
meat on Friday! Still the people come, and
for the sake of the good Samaritan's oil and
wine listen to exhortation about the need of
all sinners coming to have their souls healed at
the hands of the Great Physician. A low and
ignorant Romanist may risk little when he
abuses a mere evangelist; he will hesitate
ere he molests the medical missionary. The
kindness of the Christian surgeon is of too
precious a kind to be lightly valued.

The service being over, the presiding surgeon and his assistant retreat into the consulting room, a sanctum into whose precincts
the patients are admitted singly, the signal
to each in turn being the ringing of a table-
bell. It will be as well to sit awhile and
watch the examining and advising business
as it progresses, for by so doing we shall
learn more about the needs, and the sins

too, of a proverty-stricken district, and of blessings springing from the working of a noble society, than could be done by any other means. We will take a place at the table, in the meantime keeping our friend company who has the large ledger and his pen ready to note anything about old cases, and to enter others. The superintendent, who has been favouring us with a few words of explanation, is now in readiness also—seated in an arm chair of some dignity, as becomes a medical oracle who respects his office. Ring the bell.

The bell rings, and the door is opened slowly, as by a reverent hand, and forthwith there enters a middle-aged man, wearing a rather woe-begone expression on his countenance. The occasion of his concern is no secret: his chest is faulty and his frame is shaken by that racking cough. He may not have been indifferent while listening a few

minutes ago to what was spoken about the
healing power of the Physician of souls; but
the man's intensity of desire to be benefited
medically is absolutely painful to behold!
How minutely and carefully he answers en-
quiries! How his eyes are strained to catch
a favourable opinion in the physician's face!
Does pain hinder his sleeping at nights? Oh,
yes, yes; but not so badly as it did; no, no,
it is not quite so bad as it was. A few words
in an undertone are spoken to our near neighbour, the clerk with the ledger, and the patient
receives an order for the dispensary. He
seems to leave the room with far less gloom
than he brought in. A doctor's kind words
are as valuable as medicine. One might almost believe that a dose of good spirits had
been surreptitiously administered to this lately
depressed invalid. A good beginning. Ring
the bell.

The bell rings. This time the door opens

to admit a stout slatternly woman of the unmistakable Cowgate type. To look at her casually you might be tempted to believe the last spark of womanliness had long since been extinguished in her heart. What leaden-looking eyes! What bleared and . sottish features! Her face carries traces of recent physical suffering; but, hopelessly degraded as she appears at first sight, a second and more charitable inspection shows that there lingers in her mind a genuine feminine shyness. She is averse to being too communicative on the origin of her ailment. Something has happened of which she is ashamed. She complains of soreness and of a sharp pain in the left side, from which she has suffered since Saturday evening. The doctor has his suspicions of the cause; but anon the woman's wincing and long-drawn sighs show that the examining hand has found a fractured rib!

'Had you been drinking?' enquires the gentleman.

'A wee bit, I had,' replies the woman, in self-accusing tones, such as I am glad to hear.

Here follow a few words on the evils and dangers attending the dissolute and drink-abandoned life so common to the Cowgate. Then the poor victim departs with an order on the dispensary, and an aching side, which, it is hoped, will testify more forcibly than verbal arguments against the evils of whiskey. Ring the bell.

The bell rings, and ushers in a mother and daughter. The woman, a middle-aged body, shows a mother's anxiety written on her face for the young thing who keeps close to her natural protector with that shyness common to childhood in the presence of a doctor. The poor little patient is debarred from society and excluded from school on account of being afflicted with skin disease

over the head of an extremely rare type. The
sight presented is a spectacle sufficiently dis-
gusting to the mere visitor; but it is sure to
possess extraordinary attractions for the medical
gentlemen present, because of its rarity. The
casual visitor may turn away his head, or
hold his hat before his eyes, to spare qua-
vering nerves; the others gather round, bend
over, observe and criticise the symptoms with
a keen interest and readiness becoming men
whose art is healing, and who must gather
knowledge as they go along. I am given
to understand that it is an exceedingly interesting case — a most rare and perfect
example! Non-medical as I am, I cordially
concur in these opinions, though unable to
share my companions' curiosity. Indeed, I
am somewhat relieved to hear the superintendent say, 'Put on your hat, my dear,' to
the afflicted maiden, who looks as though she
could not quite comprehend why she should

excite so much apparent admiration. An order for admission to the infirmary is, in this case, indispensable. In the meantime the heavy-hearted mother walks away, with some gratitude warming her heart for the helping hand of the Medical Mission. But enough. Ring the bell.

The bell rings, and we have before us a young man whose constitution has been shaken by adverse influences. He looks as though he had been a subject of dissipation, but we cannot be certain, and may not judge. He may be reduced by misfortune; he may be even now repenting of past errors. We can only yield him our sympathy, and take notice of that same painful eagerness to be benefited observable in others who have passed before us. He takes an order to the dispensary, and again the bell rings its peremptory summons, while our superintendent rises from his consulting chair to welcome a brother surgeon who has just now entered.

A short, dark-featured, sharp-eyed Irish-woman walks from the inner room, her principal costume consisting of an old snuff-coloured gown and a dirty nightcap. In a room hard by this woman has a bedridden mother, who lies not only in extreme weakness, but endures much pain. The daughter has come for medicine and advice, and complains a little of her mother's restlessness. Look now in her face, and read — what? If her features speak at all, do they not say, 'Ah, it is a heavy cross when an active body has to nurse and work for a worn-out old relative'?

Perhaps the young man at my elbow is reading something of this sort in the woman's face, for he glances up from his great ledger, and remarks, drily,—

'You are not kind to her.'

What is that the gentleman is saying? Not

kind to a poor bedridden mother?   The little
Irishwoman's dark eyes sparkle with an indignation we are as gratified to see as we were
pleased to discover a few minutes ago some
embers of shame in this woman's broken-ribbed
neighbour.   There is at least a remnant of
humanity left when eyes can speak like that,
and flash an unwelcome insinuation back in
your teeth, even though they are speaking
falsely.   The transgressor who is subject to
shame is still sensible of the presence of evil.
This woman, for example, winces under rebuke,
and knows she has done wrong; so that, notwithstanding the whiskey and every-day depravity of this sin-abounding Cowgate, she has
not lapsed into evil beyond reclamation.   Some
part of the better nature of woman is still
preserved intact.

'Thin nobody's kind to her, if I ain't,' she
says, with a ringing emphasis, which we are
afraid does not impart truth to her words,

much as she would like to demonstrate that she has been wrongfully accused.

Stout denial, however, is of no avail. The phlegmatic gentleman at the great ledger is inexorable. His heart is steeled to resist the feminine art and copious vocabulary of the dark-eyed little Irishwoman. He actually repeats the offensive words slowly and emphatically, and does so, too, with a *nonchalance* which must be quite surprising to the woman,—

'Ah, you are not kind to her!'

'Thin nobody's kind to her, if I ain't.'

I shall not follow the dialogue that ensued. I can only hope the rebuke will tell for good; and that the unfortunate invalid, who is lying day after day, lonely and weary, in the close dingy room yonder, will gain a little extra attention, and enjoy a little more of a daughter's tenderness.

In the meantime the bell rings, rings again, and then again, and at each summons the door opens to admit from the inner room a subject of affliction, or a victim of transgression, to whom the helping hand of the Medical Mission is held out for the purpose of comforting and instructing in the way of salvation, and, if possible, of healing. We have only seen a small portion of one afternoon's work. The work goes on from day to day, from the beginning of the year to the close. Every day at two p.m. an afflicted and poverty-stricken congregation assembles at the dispensary to be spoken to about the healing power of the Gospel, and then to be called into the audience-chamber by the . tongue of the table-bell. Better than all, perhaps, the students who are trained by the kind of work I have described take up their abode at foreign stations, while others fill their places. Such are the operations of the Edinburgh Medical Mission, a society which merits the sympathy and support of the Church at large.

This Christian agency extends its influence beyond the dispensary and the daily religious service. Thousands of visits are paid annually to the sick and to poor women, while medical skill and medicine are freely given. Great at all times, the blessings dispensed appear even more manifest when a direful epidemic sweeps over the city, as happened during the earlier months of last year. In those sad days, had it not been for such an agency as this, we are told: 'Many would have sunk from sheer exhaustion for want of necessary food; many homes (if homes such wretched abodes can be called), with one, two, three, or four of the inmates stricken down with the pestilence, were destitute of every comfort—a bundle of straw on the floor for a bed, an old coarse sack for a blanket, no ventilation, no fire, and no food, no accommodation for the sufferers in the already over-crowded hospital, and with no help but what we were able to bestow—our

Medical Mission, in these circumstances, proved
a real blessing to very many.' .

Though the great value of medical missions
as evangelising agencies has long been acknowledged, the Edinburgh Society has been enabled
only very gradually to widen the basis of its
operations.　It is now about fifteen years since
possession was taken of the present dispensary
— the extinct Magdalen Hospital — and since
entering the Cowgate the influence of the
Society for good has perhaps become more
perceptible.　The premises, however, were used
as a common dispensary for some time previously to 1858, by a philanthropic physician,
who adopted this method of assisting the poor.
The young men who were then in course of
training for foreign service sought to improve
their experience and confer some benefit by
seconding the good doctor's endeavours.　This
friendly co-operation continued awhile, although
' dear old 39,' as its friends call the chapel,

was territory still quite independent of the mission committee. At length a change occurred, and the coveted station passed into the hands of its present managers, to become henceforth a part of their every-day machinery. It is now an active centre of Christian work, as well as a valued house of relief for the poorest of the city, where the best medical advice can be had for the asking.

There are many ladies found in Edinburgh who manifest a deep interest in the welfare of the Medical Mission, and who aid its operations as only true womanly natures can aid such endeavours. These visitors devote much of their time and substance to the interest of the poor, and one or another of their number may be frequently seen among the congregation at the Cowgate dispensary. While that little table-bell is ringing the patients into the consulting-room, one of these effective pleaders will sometimes remain in the inner chamber,

'to place before them a Triune Jehovah — a
Heavenly Father who cannot look upon sin.'
Is not this a thankless office? No; but it is
work requiring the tact and patience of cultured
womanliness. How should the Irish be treated?
As Romanists, the Irish would be glad to dis-
pense with Gospel teaching. The best things
one can say to them they call Protestantism,
and Protestantism they account defiling heresy.
Talk to them about Christ, and they will
answer, ' Oh, the Virgin will intercede for us!'
Thus the speaker must preserve her own self-
respect, and must do this without awakening
the superstitious bigotry of her rude constituents. Besides the Irish, however, other
characters are present whom we can regard
more lovingly. Rags, dirt, and vice have not
quite destroyed hope regarding them. They
begin to see, or think they do, something attractive in the Cross. On hearing the name
of Christ, they will look up and say, 'Ay, He

is the One to save us.' To kindle any interest in the minds of such people is at least encouraging; but while pleased at one symptom of success, perhaps the lady has her ardour damped when one shows peevishness at having time occupied by prayer. 'I've got no time for prayer!' 'No time for prayer? No time for prayer?' cries the visitor. 'One day you will have to find time for death!' Some, too, manifest an impatience common to rude natures, and so provoke a reprimand from the more peaceably inclined; *e.g.*, 'Can't you be quiet? If you don't want to listen to the lady, *we* do.' A few choice spirits who sometimes appear, and evince a genuine interest in what is said, probably find their way into one of the Cowgate mission churches. 'A friend of mine,' said one of this class, 'heard you the other day talking about these things here, and when she came home she told the whole of it to us.' 'Go and do likewise,' replies the lady.

Then there is a little girl sitting on the bench, whose love of Bible stories appears to inspire her relatives with excusable pride; for the mother whispers confidentially to her instructor, 'She will tell it all over again to-night!' There are many winning traits also found in some of the people here congregated; traits showing that even the Cowgate cannot totally destroy the heart's susceptibility of good impressions. How do we know this? Because more than once, when the little table-bell of the adjoining room has uttered its quick summons, unbidden tears have dimmed the eyes of patients little accustomed to weep. Wives, in whose hearts one might have supposed the last flicker of feminine generosity had died out long ago, have shown their appreciation of the word spoken in season. Gaunt, powerful men, too, in whose hard, vice-marred features, you might look in vain for what you would take to be sympathy, have uttered such words as 'Good-bye, ma'am; I won't forget what you have been telling us.'

A cheering instance of the power of the Gospel in reclaiming youth from the seemingly hopeless moral defilement of evil associations, came to light one Sabbath morning at the Cowgate Dispensary. It happened to be the first Sunday of November, and the beginning of the winter campaign of active service. Only a short time previously there had been an excursion into the country—a treat still fresh in the memories of both teachers and taught. After having been instructed in their separate rooms, the ragged classes were gathered in the chapel to listen to an address from one of the Medical Mission staff, and to receive copies of an ornamental card containing a brief, pointed prayer—'Lord, show me myself; Lord, show me Thyself. Give me Thy Holy Spirit.' The services being ended, the children passed out along the narrow passage

into the street. The surgeon-superintendent
was also leaving, when he observed one little
fellow yet lingering in the rear. To look at,
the boy was a perfect scarecrow, the bundle
of rags constituting his costume being retained
on his body by certain well-known contrivances,
noticeable among which was an ingenious and
plentiful use of string. One of the most ragged
of the ragged classes, he was a phenomenon
even in the Cowgate. At the moment it was
supposed that this could be no other than a
begging subject, and a feeling of impatience
came over the doctor in prospect of being im-
portuned for alms at the first meeting of the
school after the annual outing. When the
youngster approached, the teacher, involuntarily as it were, put his hand into his pocket,
as if to protect his coin, the thought meanwhile occurring, 'What'll he want?' Unconscious
of the uneasy emotions he was occasioning,
the lad came still closer; and, as if fearful

of being too bold or too confident, whispered, publican-like, in the superintendent's ear, '*I just wanted to tell you, doctor, I can't help thinking but that Jesus Christ has been kind to my soul.*' The kind physician—Dr. Burns Thomson—instantly feeling rebuked, bowed his head in silent thanksgiving as his eyes filled with tears. But had he made a mistake? He looked at the boy again. The little outcast still presented the appearance of a caricature of humanity. 'What is it, my little man?' was asked, and the speaker bent low, placing his best ear close to the Arab's lips. Still the confession was the same, as the convert repeated it with quiet satisfaction — 'I just wanted to tell you that Christ has been kind to my soul.' Never was a warrior more encouraged by tokens of victory than was the good medical missionary encouraged by that artless confession of a Cowgate Arab.

I hope that my readers will now perceive

the value in general of medical missions in crowded towns; and I hope they will learn to regard with favour the parent society at Edinburgh, which so admirably serves as a training institution. Into the innermost dens of sin-stricken districts the agents penetrate, and, with the Bible and their healing art for passports, find welcome everywhere. Many, ignorant of the Gospel or of morality, are brought into light and liberty, and frequently succour is carried to the destitute, or the reduced by misfortune, during the most trying season of life. I give an instance of every-day work from the diary of a Manchester visitor:—

'I had a patient lately, whose education and intelligence were very much beyond the common run of working people. Whenever I essayed to speak to him of Jesus he was dissatisfied. He often used to say, "Well, I don't think the same as you; we shall not agree upon that point." His principles were evidently sceptical, and at times he would hardly listen to me. The end was approaching. I asked the Lord, many times, how to reach his heart. God answered in a way I did not expect. The patient was confined to his bed, and could hardly breathe, not having strength to expectorate. One very bitter day he looked blue with the cold. On leaving him I said, "You look cold." "Yes," he replied, "I am." I turned down the bed-quilt, and found only a thin covering beneath. On passing downstairs, the children's bedroom door was open, and evidently the bed-clothing on the cots was very poor. On questioning the wife, I ascertained that some had been taken from the children's bed to cover the patient. A pair of blankets was sent in. At my next visit there was a decided change in his manner of speech. After a few words I left him, telling him to look at the fourth chapter of John's

Gospel, a few verses of which I quoted. The next time I called, to my great joy, I found he had asked his wife to read to him out of the blessed Book. We had now, *for the first time after four months' intercourse*, prayer together. This poor sinner at last saw the wondrous and mysterious love of God in Christ. On referring to his previous state of mind, he said, " The way the Gospel has been presented to me is very different to what I have experienced in times gone by. You see, I now understand what the Saviour meant in that passage of Matthew's Gospel: 'For I was an hungred, and ye gave Me meat: I was thirsty, and ye gave Me drink: I was a stranger, and ye took Me in: naked, and ye clothed Me: I was sick, and ye visited Me.'" Having to be out of town for a day, I went to see him before leaving. I told him it was probably the last time we should meet on earth. "Well, doctor," he replied, "we shall meet in heaven, before Him who died for us." The next day I received a hurried message that he was dying, and that he wished me to pray with him, and bid him farewell. On entering the room, he held out his thin hand, grasped mine, and with difficulty I released it. His wife raised him up, and we bowed in prayer, and again did this afflicted one strive to pray. His hand was held out again, and he expressed his hope to meet me in the presence of his Saviour. Less than ten minutes after leaving his bedside his soul passed away. I asked his wife what seemed to have impressed him so suddenly. "Well, doctor," she replied, "*I think it was the blankets.* He was completely broken down after that." '

'And He sent them to preach the kingdom of God and to heal the sick.' Medical missionaries copy the example of those who receive Christ's command, and therefore merit the countenance and sympathy of all who long for the conversion of the world. To such we commend the workers and the work. The Medical Mission of Edinburgh is an immense blessing to the poorest districts of the city. It is a blessing elsewhere also. A harvest of souls is being reaped in other towns of the empire; while from heathen climes tidings of suffering alleviated, and of Christian conquests won, gladden the hearts of those who look on from afar. It was a privilege to have an opportunity of inspecting this powerful philanthropic agency. It will be a reward if my readers, having their interest and sympathy awakened, put their hand to the great work.*

* Edinburgh Medical Missionary Society. President: W. Brown, Esq., F.R.C.S. Vice-Presidents: Professor Balfour and the Rev. G. D. Cullen, A.M. Treasurer: R. Ormond, Esq., M.D., 43, Charlotte Square. Secretary: B. Bell, Esq., F.R.C.S., 8, Shandwick Place. Superintendent: Rev. John Lowe, F.R.C.S., at the Students' Home, 56, George Square.

II.

SUNDAY NIGHT IN THE COWGATE.

19 *

SUNDAY NIGHT IN THE COWGATE.

WHILE ranking among the most interesting of cities, Edinburgh may be said to be a world in itself. The situation is romantic, the society is refined, the majority of the tradespeople are well-informed, and the historical associations of the town are so remarkable that no genial-minded Englishman grudges the proud capital of the north her self-asserting title of 'The Modern Athens.' We do not pass a mere compliment when we say that ancient Greece never rose to be half so attractive as modern Scotland.

Having something to say about the experience of a Sabbath evening which I recently spent in the lowest parts of the city, I shall preface my sketch by briefly referring to Sabbath morning, as it is observed in the more respectable districts.

It is related of a distinguished English statesman, who was staying in a Scotch village, that he expressed high satisfaction on beholding the Christian union which apparently everywhere reigned. The parish was orderly and sober, and all seemed to be of one mind as they met regularly to worship God in the Free Church. 'I suppose you have no Dissenters here?' remarked the gentleman to the church - keeper. Dissenters! Oh, yes, there were *some* Dissenters. There were at least half a dozen specimens of that discontented genus, and they might be found at the Established Church over the way! This intimation, accompanied by a significant jerk of the thumb over the speaker's shoulder, at once showed the visitor what kind of delusion he had harboured.

This anecdote will illustrate the state of religious parties in Edinburgh, and, indeed, throughout Scotland generally. While the majority of the better sort of people adhere to the Free Church, and stoutly defend her claims, the outsiders, as they may truthfully be called, belong to the State-provided Establishment; but all, in common, are subject to a strong love of Presbyterianism. Between ten and eleven o'clock on Sabbath morning the streets of the town present a spectacle such as we believe cannot be witnessed in England. The thoroughfares are thronged with passengers, grave and thoughtful, all making their way to their respective places of worship. Then the clocks chime eleven. The streets are empty. The churches are full.

One Sunday, last January, being a stranger

in Edinburgh, I walked to 'Free Saint George's,' which, as the cathedral of the Free Church of Scotland, has its pulpit occupied by Dr. Candlish, a divine who deservedly occupies a foremost place among the leaders of theological thought. The elegant and spacious edifice is receiving a broad stream of people, reminding one of the crowds which find their way into one or two of the largest of our London chapels. The congregation, too, is quite worthy of the church, including, as it does, the *élite* of the city population. The numbers who are passing in carry a thoughtful and devout look with them, and one celebrity and then another can be recognised among them. Meanwhile, the plates at the doors, standing on little tables with spotless napkins, become piled with coins, as though a special collection were being made, instead of the usual Sabbath offering. Now the people are seated; there is a hush as the Doctor ascends the pulpit, and we are eagerly anticipating the sermon. Dr. Candlish is doubtless what the Puritans would have called 'a solid and painful preacher;' and looking round, one can discern at a glance, in the calm and undivided attention of the great congregation, that it is mainly composed of hearers who are educated up to the exceedingly high standard of pulpit teaching which is maintained at 'Free Saint George's.'

On leaving the church, the streets are again found to be thronged with the same orderly crowds as before. I say orderly, because the absence of light conversation, laughter, or even smiles, is peculiarly observable. If the country were England, we should now be going home to dine; but there is no dinner in Edinburgh until after the second service at a quarter after two, which will close the public exercises of the day. Having seen the real cathedral of the Free Church, we now repair to the ancient sanctuary of Saint Giles, which in less happy times was the seat of a Bishop of Edinburgh. Saint Giles's is a great historical site, and as a mere building, is the largest church in the city; yet the congregation assembling within its walls and that assembling at 'Free Saint George's' so widely differ that they have little in common. The one is a congregation of the first class; the other is a congregation of the fourth class. Nevertheless, the hour spent in High Church, as Saint Giles's is also called, was one to be remembered. The service was impressive, and the sermon one to be highly appreciated, even though, while sitting in the fine old sanctuary of Knox and the Scottish Reformers, we could not but keenly realise that 'Free Saint George's' really represents the Church of the nation. Historical Saint Giles's merely retains 'the half-dozen Dissenters' of the Establishment.

Though the above may be a correct picture of respectable Edinburgh as the city appears in the earlier part of each Sabbath day, the evening will surely bring a less satisfactory experience. The church-going populace have gone home to dine, and to spend the remainder of the sacred hours in the profitable exercises prescribed by the religious customs of their country. Vulgar Edinburgh, which, to a casual observer, appears as little subject to Christianity as a colony of Hindoos or Chinese, has not been to church at all, and has no intention of going, and, accordingly, the Church must needs follow those waifs and strays who refuse to seek anything good for themselves, and press the Gospel upon their acceptance. There is no necessity to travel far from the handsome streets and squares to find subjects worthy of compassion. Looking down from an arch of George the Fourth's bridge, we obtain a view of a picturesque but squalid and riotous thoroughfare, and the inhabitants moving hither and thither might, to judge

from appearances, belong to another economy
in the universe from those with whom we associated in the morning. That picturesque
thoroughfare is the Cowgate. We will go
down and see what new phases of life are to
be met with in that unfashionable region, and
learn something of the agencies which seek
to relieve its abounding ignorance and destitution.

Being now fairly landed in the Cowgate,
and remembering our late experience, we seem
to be suddenly transported to some far-away
land, at the antipodes of the world we moved
in during the morning. To add to the melancholy discomfort of the scene, a mizzling rain
is falling, while the air is charged with effluvia
similar to that which obliged Dr. Johnson to
confess, on his arrival in the Canongate, that
he could smell the Scotch capital in the dark.
On either side of the way stand tall ancient
houses, with grimy windows, gaunt - looking

fronts, and heavy stone stairs ascending from the street, some of which must have done duty ever since those stirring days when their worn steps were trodden by heroic Covenanters and steadfast Christian confessors. The region has an altogether dark and forbidding aspect, while the evidences of the existence of a dense and unruly population are painfully manifest. Unwashed men and roystering youths swagger about the middle of the roadway, and hard-featured women are to be encountered on all sides. The whisky shops are closed because their landlords dare not trifle with Scotch law; but numbers of chandlers have their gas burning, their doors open, and, to judge by what we see, the Sabbath brings by no means a scant trade to this low, grovelling race, and their frowsy-looking stores. The children, prompted by natural instinct, have turned the street into a common playground, and the Scotch and Irish nationalities would seem to coalesce satisfactorily, so far as the juveniles are concerned; for the romping and shouting does not include too large a proportion of the quarrelsome element. There is one peculiarity however, about these children, which I have never observed in London: no sooner do we essay to speak to them, than the girls especially hie away, like frightened aborigines from a white man; imagining, perhaps, that we wish to accommodate them with places in the ragged-school or the mission chapel.

But where are we? In the Cowgate of Old Edinburgh? Yes, and in spite of the heavy atmosphere, the sickly-looking shops, and the teeming, degraded populace, let us realise that we are now treading on classical ground—that we stand among buildings which in prouder days were made to play a conspicuous part in the history of Scotland. Here was the Solemn League and Covenant drawn up and signed in 1638. Here was the young and beautiful Queen Mary entertained by admiring citizens, before troubles, preshadowing death, overtook her. And here, too, in a quaint little chapel, wherein the Medical Mission holds its weekly meetings, the first General Assembly of the Church of Scotland is said to have been held. Rich in historical association, and picturesque notwithstanding its squalor and abounding vice, is this ancient thoroughfare. Evil days and a bad reputation may have fallen upon its weather-beaten homes; but choice words of Scripture on the walls, quaintly spelt, peep out from the encrusted dirt of ages, to remind us of noble names belonging to the past, and to inspire us with the hope of seeing better days in the future.

We have now arrived at the chapel, or the Cowgate station of the Medical Mission; a building of great historical interest, dating its foundation from pre-Reformation times. Passing down a dimly-lighted, narrow passage,

and catching by the way some uncompli-
mentary remarks from divers natives, who
are watching our progress with needless
curiosity, we soon emerge into a small court-
yard, where are a number of rooms and a
dispensary, all of which in other days formed
the hospital apartments belonging to the
quaint little chapel in the front. Here the
ragged-school classes assemble on Sabbath
evenings; and the students of the Medical
Mission are now earnestly engaged in teaching
troops of little outcasts, fresh from the dens
of this dreadful Cowgate, the first principles
of Christianity. 'Barren ground!' 'Casting
pearls before swine!' we are tempted to
exclaim in our short-sighted wisdom, as we
stand watching the teachers' painful efforts.
Let us, however, be sparing of sentimentality.
God is blessing the seed so faithfully and
unsparingly sown! There is an unmistakable
Northern inquisitiveness implanted in the

young hearts before us, and the eagerness with which they listen to what is spoken is at least encouraging. The lessons for the evening are printed on large sheets, pasted on boards, each being embellished with a large engraving; and now and again, when something striking is said, the heads of a whole class bend forward to reinspect the picture and to catch the meaning of what is being explained. Perhaps the scene is as unlike a London ragged-school as Scotland is unlike England. Several of the pinched little faces carry an expression painfully striking, as if their owners were already old in vice, through being thrown among associations cruelly out of keeping with bodies so young. These we may pronounce to be the children of whiskey-drinking parents. There are others, on the contrary, whose pretty youthful features bear the stamp of childishness, while their persons are cleaner and their clothing is better

kept than is the case with their more unfortunate companions. It is a sight calculated to
make one yearn for the little creatures' welfare.
Nor shall we yearn in vain; for now the
lessons are finished we pass from the hot,
close atmosphere into the open court, feeling
that the efforts thus put forth in faith, or even
in tears, will surely be blessed by God and
yield a full return.

At half-past six a meeting will be held in
the mission chapel, when one of the medical
students will give an address; but, meanwhile,
the congregation has to be sought—literally
compelled or persuaded to come in. Though
some may scoff and refuse compliance, others
will yield, so that the assembly is quite a
motley company, full of interest to a student
of human nature. See them now gathered
together. There sits an aged Scotchman, in-
firm and afflicted, who by misfortune, perhaps,
rather than by wilful misconduct, has been

driven into the notorious locality of the Cowgate; and he appears to profit by what he hears. Near the old man is a decent, demure - looking woman in widow's weeds, who also prizes the religion of her fathers, or her features belie her heart. The sad picture has its lighter shadings, but is a melancholy study taken as a whole. The background contains nothing cheerful, being chiefly made up of a number of young men and lasses, whom to look at even makes one's heart ache with misgivings. The most promising thing in connection with them is the fact of their being found in the mission chapel at all.

One of the mission churches is also open to-night; for, as the regular services close with the afternoon, this building is used for evening lectures by the Free Church students of New College. This practice should successfully introduce ministerial candidates to an effective style of preaching. In the main it doubtless conduces to this end, though we turned from this service disappointed. As a missionary effort, the whole was a failure. The young speaker, an able classical scholar, and one read in general literature, made so ready a use of book-lore, that his sermon resembled the Gospel according to the English Poets.

There are many other evangelistic agencies in the Cowgate, which I cannot notice, but their existence and success reflect high honour on the Christian community of Edinburgh. There are ragged schools, children's services, and churches founded on Dr. Chalmers's territorial system, all reaping a precious harvest, surprising to contemplate when we recollect the nature of the ground in which the good seed is sown.

Yet, notwithstanding the marked success of the missionaries in this chosen retreat of sin, we cannot be surprised when we find the workers themselves half imagining that Christianity is losing ground in a degenerate age. It is true these brave men work and succeed, and they are persons well qualified to take a correct measure of their success; but in places exceptionally degraded, a band of Christian labourers, however successful, cannot produce an impression very visible to outside observers. They succeed in reclaiming certain numbers, and these they raise in the social scale, by engendering those higher tastes and soberer habits which always accompany religion. But what are the immediate consequences? The converts become the subjects of new desires and aspirations, and these oblige them to flee from their old quarters as from a lazaretto or a doomed City of Destruction. They almost invariably move away to respectable neighbourhoods, while new-cómers as surely fill up the vacancies in the common haunt, to invite in turn the attention of the mission pastors. This is what is continually happening in the territorial churches of the Cowgate and Westport; and Mr. Pirie, of the former place, assured me that he expected it would so continue till the end of his days.

It may be in a sense disheartening to hard-working men, whose lot is cast in a low and degraded neighbourhood, to see their converts move off to swell the roll of prosperous churches; but none the less does the general result, so far as this one vicinity is concerned, appear to be magnificent. Into one mission church in the Cowgate no less than two thousand persons have been received in about a dozen years, and two hundred and ten of the number were admitted during the past year. Nearly the whole of these have been fairly drawn from the native populace—have, in reality, been won for Christ on one of Satan's most fiercely-contested battle-fields. True indeed it is that the fair city of Edinburgh, like our own great London, does not and cannot know herself, while about a third part of her two hundred thousand inhabitants refuse

even to enter the places set apart for the worship
of God.   On this account do we sympathise with
the misgivings of some in the face of abounding
difficulties.   Would any learn what these difficulties are?   Let them watch the faces and
catch the conversation of an Edinburgh mob
when aught exciting draws them together, and
they will have a study of human nature as appalling as our empire can supply.   A place like
the Cowgate, where outcasts herd together in
surprising numbers, is an intricate network of
dens as closely packed as cells in a honeycomb.
Stand for a minute in one of the closes, and
remember that a population as large as a
moderate village dwell in that confined area!
Nay, further; in the rooms approached by one
flight of stairs, between two and three hundred
wretched beings have been found crowding
together in shocking indecency, without a ray
of hope either for this world or the next!   The
most commonplace necessaries of life are never

theirs. They do not know what enjoyment means! There are sinners here who have forgotten, or who never knew, the difference between right and wrong! Virtue could not preserve her purity untarnished for an hour in their pestiferous haunts! As though prompted by the demon of despair, these poor creatures seek to deaden the pain of their monotonous misery by swallowing the vile cheap whiskey which is sold at their very doors—and sold, perhaps, by their own heartless landlord, who feeds like a vampire on the degradation and final ruin of his helpless tenants and customers.

The Rev. John Pirie's mission church in the Cowgate now numbers nine hundred members, nearly a fourth part of whom have been added during one year. It was agreeably surprising to find that so fine a mission station is fast becoming self-supporting; for, while we scarcely comprehend how persons who possess

' one half-crown to rub on the back of another '
can live in so notorious a rookery, the pastors
do not complain of any painful lack of money
among the populace. On the contrary, money
must abound, when more than thirty spirit
shops are liberally supported in one street.
Though it is not easy to say whence the money
comes, it seems obvious that many persons of
stations in life superior to the locality are con-
tent to live in the lowest parts of Edinburgh.
Printers, compositors, and skilled workmen,
whose families should be the pride of better
homes, are found neighbouring with Scotch
cadgers and Irish hodmen. Such is the varied
constituency; and we honour the men who, like
Mr. Pirie in the Cowgate, and Mr. Tasker in the
Westport, have taken up their position and are
devoting time and talent to the highest service.
This they do, not as evangelists merely, but as
ordained pastors, qualified and selected for work
peculiarly arduous. They are pastors, too, whose

preaching powers—to judge from a sample we heard in the Westport church — might be coveted by the most wealthy churches of the city.

In the low parts of Edinburgh Old Town public-houses and pawn-shops abound; and these appear to work in unison, if we may judge from the number of pledges which whiskey-slaves are constantly offering in their mad eagerness for stimulants. More than eighty spirit-shops may be counted during a walk from Holyrood to the Castle, and many hundreds of others exist in the various districts of the city. I learned that as many as eleven thousand pledges have been taken at one pawning establishment in a single month in the beginning of the year, the articles including trinkets, books, clothing, and household furniture. I even heard of a Bible having been snatched from the pillow of a poor invalid, to procure money for purchasing spirits! I heard further of a man, whose wife had so repeatedly pawned his Sabbath clothes in order to gratify her craving for drink, that at length, to save his garments, he resorted to the necessary but inconvenient expedient of changing the suit for another at a neighbour's, each Sunday evening before returning home. In such an atmosphere childhood is contaminated before it can know the meaning of either virtue or sin. Even children learn to become drunkards, and unless they are rescued in time—especially the girls—they pass swiftly onward to reinforce the ranks of crime and immorality.

In these lurking-places of sin the children must form the basis of our hopes for the future; and the crowded condition of the children's church leads us to anticipate reformation and renovation for these abodes of squalor and vice. It is easy to see at a glance that there are many rough gems among the Edinburgh Arabs. A vein of humour runs through their nature, which may be either amusing or annoying, obliging those who know them best to tell us that they are characterised by 'a matchless impudence.' They are, however, willing learners and eager readers, so that, considering the amount of trash they devour while lacking wholesome literary food, it will be well when the asked-for library is provided. Some of the children have curious histories — histories which show that philanthropic feeling can live even in the Cowgate. 'It is years now since,' says Mr. Pirie, 'visiting in one of the closes, I entered a humble abode, the dwelling-place of a poor but honest and hard-working family. While I was conversing with the mother, a little girl entered the room, apparently from school, and commenced a meal which was awaiting her. I asked if this was her daughter, and the woman told me that she was not. The mother of that child had been a stranger, and without an earthly home. In the house of that poor family the wanderer had sickened and died, leaving the poor child without a friend on earth; and this woman, out of the goodness of her own heart, spread her own wing over the little orphan, and for years had been unto her as her mother. Perhaps she did more than any of us all.'*

Any person acquainted with the poor localities of other cities, will pronounce the Edinburgh Cowgate to be as vile a collection of dens as can be found in the empire. The pastors who have spent some of their best days here can testify to the 'almost savage degradation' which everywhere confronts one, and which, notwithstanding the success of the mission churches, compels the evangelists, in their fits of despondency, to shed tears of despair, and to regard their territory as 'a

* See Mr. Pirie's timely pamphlet, 'The Lapsed; and Suggestions as to the best Means of Raising them.' (Edinburgh: John Maclaren.)

God-forsaken soil.' No nation should boast of its civilisation while such plague-spots remain. 'When death cuts off a member of the family,' says Dr. Begg, speaking of these localities, 'how dreadful to think of all the rest being forced to eat and sleep beside the dead body! We drag a dead horse out of the stable of the living; but here such a separation is impossible. How can we wonder that human nature, in such circumstances, is found at the lowest point of degradation, defying the ordinary modes of cure, and spreading moral as well as physical evil like a pestilence! A decent man comes from the country, driven, perhaps, by want of work. He is obliged to live in one of these wretched abodes. Let us suppose that he has been accustomed to the decencies of society, or even that he is a true Christian. How dreadful to have his children, like Lot in Sodom, exposed to the sound of blasphemy, and the example of every form of wickedness! There society is corrupted to its very core. City missionaries go their rounds in despair. Oceans of soup and floods of water are lavished in vain. The managers of infirmaries, the keepers of prisons, the masters of charity workhouses, stand aghast at a tide flowing from such a corrupted mass, and which, instead of being driven back, is continually rising, like the prophetic waters, and threatening to sweep away all that is sound and healthy in the community.'

As we pass along in the mizzling rain, the heavy flights of stone stairs look as if they had been made privy to suffering and shame, as well as to deeds of sin, dark and horrible, which will remain untold till the last day! Besides being dark and filthy, the passages are a common receptacle for the refuse of the rooms. 'Think now,'. says our missionary, ' of a family of nine, ten, and sometimes twelve, and in not a few instances more than *one* such family, doomed to dwell day and night, to eat, drink, lie down, sleep, and rise up, and perform all their domestic duties in an apartment smaller than an ordinary dressing closet!' Sometimes a clean room is discovered, and when found is as refreshing to the visitor as an oasis to travellers in the desert. But none can, with impunity, live clean and moral lives in this dreadful place; and those who try to do so will tell the evangelist, with troubled looks, of the annoyances which spring from the drunken revelries of profligate neighbours. Be you as orderly as you will, you cannot have either peace or repose at pleasure in the Cowgate; for, as if purposely designed to reduce all its inhabitants to one level of ruin, the house-partitions are so slight that the foul conversation spoken in one room can be plainly heard in another. Many a life has been wrecked here beyond hope of recovery! It is a region which awakens at once our pity, sorrow, and indignation—a very devil's acre, where, having planted their standard and marshalled their hosts, the demons Crime and Despair successfully defy and resist the menaces and assaults of Christian Scotland.

Such was the Edinburgh Cowgate in the month of January, 1873. A more 'graphic' delineation of its miseries and character might have been attempted had such been my design, but I have preferred keeping to unvarnished, simple truth, for the sake of stimulating those who are working, and encouraging others to aid the good cause who have as yet held aloof. Whence has the broad torrent of evil, at which we have been looking, its spring? Was there ever an infernal conclave held to select a subtle agent to subject and hold this seemingly-doomed place in captivity? If so, the demon WHISKEY must have stood up to demand a commission. 'Send me!' Drunkenness is the master-curse of the Scotch capital, and will continue so while the city harbours eight hundred public-houses, or one to each two hundred of the population! 'Fancy,' again says our missionary, 'thirty-one spirit-shops —some of them in threes continuously—in a small street like the Cowgate, over against its two Protestant churches, and the revenues of each of the spirit shops that of the church perhaps three times over!' We might stand unnerved and helpless in the presence of such enormous evils, did not faith find reassurance in the grand fact that the battle is not ours, but God's.

An Englishman who first walks out into the streets of Edinburgh speedily discovers that whiskey is a leading article of commerce in the city. I was even given to understand that the poor regard beer very much as a luxury, and retain the spirits as an every-day beverage. The populace suffer severely by their pernicious predilections. Nay, what is more important, sanitary reformers are directly tracing the relationship between disease, vagrancy, and crime, and the drinking customs of the people, since the poor of Scottish cities delight in vile concoctions doled out to them as genuine spirits, or 'Our celebrated Toddy Mixture' at one shilling and ninepence per bottle. For a long time past the excessive mortality of Glasgow has occasioned perplexity and even alarm among philanthropists and well-to-do citizens, and very praiseworthy have been the efforts made to lower the frightful death-rate. It has been in vain, however; and recently the local newspapers have been using severe language towards one sanitary reformer who professes to have discovered in spirit-drinking a fountain which stimulates the growth of hot-beds of fever. Looking at the question from the temperance rather than from the teetotal standpoint, I confess to having been appalled by the figures and conclusions of this 'teetotal child,' as his opponents style the gentleman referred to. In one part of the city of Glasgow, where the doomed inhabitants herd thickly together in close, damp courts, and where a spirit-shop flourishes for each eight score people, as many as eleven per cent. of the inhabitants were stricken by fever in a single year! I do not infer that this horrible state of affairs has its spring solely in drunkenness; but a continuous consumption of raw, inferior spirit, by an underfed populace, must be attended by fatal results. Cheap fiery liquors are poisons which quickly and effectively complete their deadly work, so that to dispute the ground with the evils arising from their use does not merely belong to Good Templars and other teetotal clubs. It is the legitimate work of the Christian Church in common, and in few places is this realised so keenly as in Edinburgh.

In the meantime, the great work of renovation progresses, while we, perhaps, are asking in perplexity, only relieved by faith, What shall be done to reclaim such moral wastes as the Cowgate and the Canongate — the fatal retreats of every ill which oppresses human nature? Fanciful descriptions of the 'Special Commissioner' class serve to amuse, but yield no substantial fruit. Indeed, 'graphic' exaggerations of the misfortunes and miseries of the indigent and fallen have too often given offence to the people directly referred to. Such writing seldom tends towards reformation. What, then, shall be done to raise these myriads of our brethren and our sisters in Edinburgh, to whom the most commonplace requisites of civilisation are unknown luxuries? First, the localities absolutely require to be razed to the ground, so that proper buildings may be erected. Our evangelists labour under cruel disadvantages when standing in the presence of a mass of squalor and disease, which a corps of masons and labourers could, in a great measure, speedily remove. Clean dwellings—or dwellings which might be clean at the will of the inmates—are indispensable. Would we could hail the dawn of those better days which we long to see! Light, water, and pure air are not so expensive or scarce but that all might enjoy them. It is almost heart-breaking work to persons of fine Christian instinct, when they have to speak of Christ and of moral duties in dirty rooms opening into dark, loathsome passages, where the air is tainted by the refuse which chokes up the corners or even obstructs the pathway. Replacing ancient rotten buildings by decent houses is, after all, not a task of superlative difficulty. Such a work is actually going forward, though more slowly than the urgency of the case demands. Private beneficence is doing a little, and city corporations are doing something also. According to common report, Mr. Ruskin achieved a noble triumph some years ago under this head. He purchased a dilapidated pile of tenements, which a former landlord had complacently relinquished to the reign of moral disorder and physical disease. On passing into the possession of their new owner, the houses were completely renovated, thoroughly repaired, and made in all respects convenient, or even attractive. Then a woman blessed with a knowledge of domestic matters was appointed overseer as well as rent collector; and this matron did her part in teaching such of the occupants as chose to become pupils something about cooking, and the science of housewifery in general. What some have thus done in a small way, we want to see done on a larger scale. Not until such works are earnestly taken in hand, shall we have a ready answer when confronted with such an appalling enigma as, What shall be done to diminish the savage degradation and suffering of places like this ancient Canongate and historically-renowned Cowgate? We can provide an army of missionaries brave and enterprising; but why should the devoted band be ever missing their mark, wasting moral force, and hazarding failure, when a corps of sappers and miners could prepare them a way which would lead to an easier victory? Those who will provide better dwellings for the poor in great cities can by so doing aid evangelistic work in an important degree. More than this: we see no reason why owners of fever-breeding haunts should not be compelled by law to replace by creditable habitations those piles of rotten tenements which disgrace our civilisation, and in which the moral instincts of the young are blunted before they can know what religion or morality means.

UNWIN BROTHERS, PRINTERS, CHILWORTH AND LONDON.